ALSO BY ERIC PUCHNER

Music Through the Floor

Model Home

LAST
DAY ON
EARTH

- stories -

ERIC PUCHNER

SCRIBNER

New York   London   Toronto   Sydney   New Delhi

Scribner
An Imprint of Simon & Schuster, Inc.
1230 Avenue of the Americas
New York, NY 10020

First Scribner hardcover edition February 2017

For information about special discounts for bulk purchases, please contact Simon & Schuster Special Sales at 1-866-506-1949 or business@simonandschuster.com.

The Simon & Schuster Speakers Bureau can bring authors to your live event. For more information or to book an event, contact the Simon & Schuster Speakers Bureau at 1-866-248-3049 or visit our website at www.simonspeakers.com.

Interior design by Jill Putorti

Manufactured in the United States of America

10 9 8 7 6 5 4 3 2 1

Library of Congress Cataloging-in-Publication Data is available.

ISBN 978-1-5011-4780-7
ISBN 978-1-5011-4782-1 (ebook)

Versions of these stories have previously appeared elsewhere: "Brood X" (*Narrative*); "Beautiful Monsters" (*Tin House, Best American Short Stories,* and *Best American Nonrequired Reading*); "Mothership" (*Tin House*); "Independence" ("Bookstories from *McSweeney's*"); "Heavenland" (*Zyzzyva*); "Trojan Whores Hate You Back" (*Tin House*); "Right This Instant" (*Epoch*); "Last Day on Earth" (*Granta*).

For Katharine

Ploffskin, Pluffskin, Pelican jee!
We think no birds so happy as we!
Plumpskin, Ploshkin, Pelican jill!
We think so then, and we thought so still!

—EDWARD LEAR

CONTENTS

LAST
DAY ON
EARTH

BROOD X

It was the summer of the cicadas. They'd been living underground for seventeen years, but now they tunneled out of the earth and climbed the trees and telephone poles, breaking free of their bodies and sprouting wings. They left their old selves clinging to branches, like perfect glass replicas. Overnight, it seemed, the ancient oaks bubbled and seethed and turned into enormous growths of coral. Dogs went crazy, digging in the dirt and gobbling up white nymphs by the dozens. The sidewalks shimmered like streams. We collected shells in our shirts and made necklaces that we wore around like witch doctors. The wings were amazing things, veined and delicate as a fairy's, and we harvested them from corpses or plucked them from still-buzzing cicadas in order to frighten girls. The bugs rarely took flight, but our neighbor, Mrs. Palanki, refused to leave the house without her umbrella, running to the car with her head ducked down, as if pummeled by rain.

This was in Guilford, a wealthy section of Baltimore, where summers usually consisted of badminton and touch football in the street and endless pickled mornings of blindman's bluff in the pool. We'd run home every day for BLTs. The strangest thing that happened was the occasional bat inside the house.

But now the cicada noise was so deafening we had to yell at each other to be heard. Outside it was like a train roaring by. The insects themselves were black and ugly, with beady orange eyes that looked like fish eggs. Everywhere—in the trees, on gutter spouts, on the bill of someone's cap—they seemed to be growing second heads. It took us a while to figure out what was going on. They fastened themselves together, wings enfolded, so that you couldn't tell where one bug ended and the other began.

"Screwing," Stefano Giordano shouted. He was thirteen, a year older than me, and an authority on sex. The cicadas were smooshed together on the windowsill outside his bedroom. The rest of us gathered around.

"No way," I said.

"That's what my dad said. The male dies right after, and the female lays her eggs in a tree."

We were skeptical until we saw it happen: the slow uncoupling, then the one buzzing off somewhere while the other remained on the windowsill. After a while it dropped to the ground and its little legs began to curl up. I had never really watched something die before. It was slow and punctilious and kind of a letdown. I kept thinking how the bug was older than I was, yet had only gotten to see the world for a few days.

In the middle of the noise and chaos of the cicadas that summer a new family moved into our neighborhood. They'd come from California, we heard, and I can't imagine what they must have thought of their new home. We watched from our bikes as the movers unloaded their things, crunching through the cicada shells at their feet. It was miserably humid, and furniture kept slipping out of the movers' hands. One of them, cursing in a foreign language, threw a tennis ball at the maple tree in the front yard, and for a moment the sky was like a popcorn popper swirling with bugs.

The next day my mom baked some brownies, and I walked with her under the frantic buzzing oaks. The house our new neighbors had moved into was an old Victorian, smaller than ours, with a peeling front porch and gabled windows popping out from the roof. The previous owner, Mrs. Winters, had died several years before and bequeathed it to her only daughter, who'd let it go vacant before deciding to move in herself. In the time it lay empty the house had become a favorite topic of my mother, who liked to speculate on what it looked like inside. Normally a lovely and compassionate woman, she took a devout interest in the deterioration of other people's homes. *What, pray tell, have the Morrisons done to their kitchen?* she'd ask at dinner, pausing over her Brussels sprouts, or, *The Sieglers have really let their garden go to pot.*

She rang the bell, and Mrs. Winters's daughter answered the door, dressed in a tunic with little paisleys on it, her long ferny lashes seeming to stick together for a second when she blinked at us. She looked, I thought, like the sort of woman a movie monster might snatch from a crowd. At thirty-five, my mother was one of the younger parents on the block, but watching her greet our new neighbor I felt for the first time that she was old. The woman introduced herself—Karen Jennings was her name—and stared past us at an icicle of cicadas hanging from a nearby oak.

My mother made a face. "Hideous, aren't they?"

"Oh, I don't know. Something kind of fabulous about them, don't you think?" Mrs. Jennings closed her eyes for a moment, as if listening to the trees. "They certainly make your life, um, biblical."

My mom tried to smile at her and peer into the house at the same time. I had never heard anyone's mother talk like this before, describe a plague of insects as "fabulous." A thrill breezed through me. As I ducked out from under my mother's hand, a boy who looked about my age came to the door with something jutting from his lips. A cigarette. Little shreds of tobacco poked out of the crumpled tip. My mother stopped craning her neck to see inside and took a step backward.

"This is JJ," Mrs. Jennings said.

"Jules, Mom."

"*Jules,*" she said, rolling her eyes.

My mom was staring at the boy's lips. "Where did you get that cigarette?"

"I'm not actually smoking," he said without taking it from his mouth.

"It's just for fun," Mrs. Jennings said. "In his case, at least. I'm in it to the grisly end."

The boy plucked the cigarette from his lips and wedged it behind his ear. I did not like the looks of him. He had freckles like me, except he was skinny and frizzy-haired and wearing long pants—corduroys—in the middle of summer. Plus he had something wrong with his eye. One of his pupils had a black line spoking out from it, like the hand of a watch stuck at six o'clock. He caught me staring at it, I think, because he turned away and went back inside the house. It seemed impossible to me that this freaky kid and gorgeous mother were related.

My mother hesitated when Mrs. Jennings invited us in for some coffee, but her curiosity got the best of her and I followed her into the Jenningses' house, which was still lined with boxes. There were paintings everywhere, leaning against some of the weirdest furniture I'd ever seen. One chair looked like a bunch of curtain rods with a strip of brown-spotted hide stretched across them, as if a lunatic had tried to make a trampoline out of a cow. I couldn't resist touching it as I passed. Mrs. Jennings took the brownies from my mother and served them on plates that didn't match, along with something that looked like ice cubes rolled in pink powder. "Turkish delight," she called the cubes, explaining how she'd ordered them from a shop in the East Village. I didn't know what the East Village was, but my mom's expression said that it was a place she didn't care for.

Chewing on a cube, whose deliciousness surprised me, I wandered over to a painting leaning against the far wall, an eerie desert scene with a circular forest in the middle of it surrounded by a fence. In the foreground, stretching toward the forest, was an animal I didn't recognize. It was strange and horrible-looking, something like a hairless zebra but with its head sprouting vertically from its neck and a little tadpole mouth. It didn't have any ears. Looking closer, I saw that the opening to the forest was framed by a pair of enormous female legs, spread like the giant doors of a gate.

"That's the sex painting," Jules said to me, checking to see we were out of earshot.

"Sex?"

"See, it's a giant penis. And that's supposed to be a vagina. It's surrealist. One of my dad's friends painted it."

I inspected it with deeper interest. Above the sex painting, perched on the mantel, was a framed photograph of a dapper-looking man with a sunburned nose. It was a large, handsome, mesmerizing nose, and probably often sunburned. No photos but this one had been unpacked—at least that I could see.

"Where's your dad?" I asked. "At work?"

"He's dead."

The way he said this, eyes fixed to the floor, made me stop asking questions. While my mother updated Mrs. Jennings on the neighborhood and the history of its poorly maintained homes, Jules offered to show me his room, then surprised me by taking me down a long flight of stairs to the basement. A lightbulb dangled from the ceiling, flickering on and off like a ship's. Jules led me through the dank cellar to his room, which smelled of fresh paint. The only decoration was a single poster, one of those space pictures of a galaxy abloom with color, the sort of thing I imagined you might see on your way to the afterlife.

"That's the Cigar Galaxy," Jules said. "Messier Eighty-two." He sounded bored, as if anyone with half a brain would know what the Cigar Galaxy was. He took the cigarette from his ear and tweezed it between two fingers, like someone on TV. "Are you familiar with the multiverse?"

"The what?"

"The multiverse. Like our universe is just one of trillions of universes out there. Commonly known as the many-worlds interpretation."

"That's stupid," I said.

6

"My dad's a physicist. *Was.* He told me all about it." He pointed his cigarette at my chest. "Probability-wise, there's a parallel universe out there where you and I are talking right now, exact same conversation, everything, but you're wearing a green shirt instead of a blue one."

I looked down at my shirt. I was starting to feel a little funny. I'd never heard a twelve-year-old use expressions like "probability-wise" before. This was 1987, before the World Wide Web, before loony ideas were as prevalent as the cicadas buzzing outside. I was beginning to feel trapped under the earth.

"The possibilities are literally infinite," Jules said. He narrowed his eyes. "If you've learned to navigate them."

"What the hell are you talking about?"

"I'm saying that navigation is possible." He leaned into me, and his face was suddenly leering. "What girl would you most like to fuck?"

The word startled me. I had the impression it was the first time he'd ever said it out loud. "Phoebe Merchant," I said, then immediately regretted it. I didn't know why I'd confessed this to him— perhaps because no one had ever asked me so bluntly. Phoebe was the girl who lived across the street. She had long black hair she could wrap around her neck like a noose and braces on her teeth, which kept my hopes tragically alive. Sometimes Stefano Giordano and I would walk down to the racquet club and spy on her as she played tennis, staring at the pink sunrise of her underpants as she bent over to wait for a serve.

"There's a universe out there, believe it or not, where you're nailing her brains out."

Jules opened a door beside his desk and revealed a room with a folding chair in it and lots of cobwebby shelves built into the walls. A root cellar, he called it. He told me to go inside and sit down. Maybe because he'd impressed me with the word "fuck," I obeyed him. There was a stash of crumpled-looking cigarettes on a paper plate on the floor, as if he spent a lot of time sitting in there by himself.

No sooner had I sat in the chair than Jules closed the door. I rattled the knob, but he'd locked it somehow and it wouldn't turn.

"Let me out of here!"

"Relax and try to enjoy the trip. Of course, you can't think of it like travel. More like diving underwater and coming back up in a different place."

"I'll kill you!" I said. I began to kick the door.

"Stop doing that," he said pleasantly, "or I'll erase you from the earth."

I stopped. It was dark, but my eyes were adjusting to it and the corners of the root cellar began to reverse themselves into existence. I pressed my ear against the door but couldn't hear much of anything, just a faint rhythmic humming, what I imagined to be the roar of the cicadas outside. Maybe it was because of the dark, or because I was inside where the noise didn't belong, but the sound seemed to emanate from my own brain. I wondered if Jules had left the bedroom. Perhaps he'd tell everyone I went home. I'd be locked up in the root cellar forever, starving to death while the police scoured the city, rotting at long last into a pile of bones. *Pharaoh pharaoh pharaoh*, the cicadas sang. To keep from panicking, I closed my eyes and tried to imagine what I'd look like in a different universe, one where girls fell miraculously at my feet. I would not have freckles all over my arms. My hair would not be red. It would be brown, like my brother's, and

I wouldn't be embarrassed by how pale I was every time I had to be Skins during soccer practice.

When Jules opened the door he was smiling. It was a weird smile, curled around his cigarette as if he were trying to keep himself from eating it. My hands were shaking. I pushed him as hard as I could and he sprawled across the floor, the cigarette flying out of his mouth, but the smile didn't leave his face.

That evening at dinner, my mom couldn't stop talking about the Jenningses' house. She seemed particularly interested in the cigarette dangling from Jules's mouth, which she blamed entirely on Mrs. Jennings. To me the cigarette seemed unique proof that the kid was deranged, but to my mother it was somehow connected to the paintings and the cow furniture and the mismatched plates. She had always seemed fearless to me—once, when we were camping in Canada, she'd scared away a bear with a canoe paddle—so it was weird to hear her recount these details so obsessively, holding them up like treacherous, snapping things.

"And she served these horrible pink sweets," my mother said, ignoring the plate of meatloaf in front of her. "Turkish delights. I couldn't help noticing she didn't eat any herself."

My father, for his part, seemed to accept my mother's judgment. He was an internist at the hospital and grateful enough that my mom had dinner waiting when he came home, treating each incarnation of stroganoff or turkey Tetrazzini as if it were the Second Coming of Christ. He'd close his eyes as he ate and tell her she was the best "chef" in Maryland. On his days off he liked to shoot things out of

the sky and bring them home for my mother to clean. Our freezer
was a necropolis of birds. When he wasn't shooting things, he horsed
around with us in the backyard or tried to play catch, though he
treated it like an amusingly absurd game he had no real interest in.
Eventually he would drift off and take his hunting dogs out of the
kennel, two German shorthaired pointers who froze into trembling
statues at the sight of an animal. He spent hours running them up and
down the yard. My father may have felt guilty for spending so much
time with his dogs, or for all those ducks and pheasants my poor
mother had to pluck, because he was always telling her how beautiful she was, a source of enduring mortification to me. Sometimes he
whispered in her ear and she giggled in a way that made me want to
untie my shoes so I could focus on tying them again. Theo, my older
brother, called these displays "child abuse." It was one thing in the
privacy of our home but quite another at, say, an Orioles game, where
they ran the risk of ending up on TV. Sometimes my father would
look at us when he flattered her, and I wondered who these lavish
displays were for. Other times he'd enter one of his "funks," as my
mother put it, retreating to his office in the attic and failing to emerge
for dinner, but we'd come to accept them—like the sour-refrigerator
smell he brought home from the hospital or the scratchy brown beard
he sometimes groomed with a little comb—as part of the unremark-
able mystery of his life.

"He's a total freak job," I said, steering the subject back to Jules. I
explained about his eye and how it looked like a little clock.

"Sounds like a coloboma of the iris," my father said, frowning. He
scratched his beard, which had begun to go a bit gray. "Benign muta-
tion, probably. Anyway, what's a freak job?"

"A person of unsound mental fitness," Theo said. At fourteen, he considered himself something of a liaison between generations. He hadn't bothered to change after lacrosse practice, and the giant shoulder pads he was wearing made his head look like a voodoo hex. "Why's he such a freak?"

I'd been thinking of the multiverse, but something—a tingle of fear—kept me from bringing it up. "He's got a picture of a woman's open legs."

"What?" my mother said.

My father seemed intrigued. "An actual picture?"

I nodded. "A zebra's about to enter them."

My mom, who clearly hadn't seen the picture, had turned white. She was looking at my father.

"It's surrealist," I explained, feeling—now that I'd seen my parents' reaction—an itch to defend it.

"I don't want you going over there again," my mother said sternly.

I glanced at the painting of a man and woman in old-fashioned clothes that hung in our dining room. They were floating in a rowboat, the woman trailing her fingers in the water while the man gripped the oars. I'd never thought much about this picture, one way or the other, but suddenly it seemed like the stupidest thing in the world.

"I'll tell you what I heard," Theo said, shaking some ketchup onto his plate. "His dad offed himself. Shot himself in their minivan. And it was the kid that found him, I guess, in the backseat."

"Who told you that?" my mother said, frowning.

Theo shrugged. "Zachary Porter."

"Zachary Porter doesn't know anything," I said, though it was only the idea of Mrs. Jennings owning a minivan that upset me.

*   *   *

Before long more rumors surfaced about Mr. Jennings: he hadn't killed himself but had been murdered; he'd been experimenting with drugs and had jumped off a roof; he'd shot himself to get away from Mrs. Jennings, who'd invented his madness in order to get to his money. The rumors were made worse by Mrs. Jennings herself, who'd begun taking aimless walks around the neighborhood in black boots that zipped up to her knees, chain-smoking her way past our yards while cicadas ratcheted above her. Even when we weren't infested with bugs, people in Guilford didn't wander around for no reason— the best theory we could come up with was that it was for her health, a form of exercise, but that didn't explain the boots and the cigarettes and the way she stopped in the middle of the sidewalk to stare up at the trees, tusks of smoke streaming from her nostrils.

Sometimes Jules would accompany her on her walks. Once, taking the trash out after dinner, I saw them stop at the sapling near the end of our driveway so that Jules could pluck a cicada off one of its leaves, pinching the thing between his fingers, where it made a sound like a windup toy when you turn the key the wrong way. He held it up to Mrs. Jennings's ear, and she laughed. How horrified my mother would be, I thought enviously.

It wasn't until the Biscoes' annual Fourth of July barbecue that I actually talked to Jules again. People stood on the lawn drinking wine coolers and sodas, doing their best to distract themselves from Brood X. This was what the newspapers were calling the cicadas. They'd be mating for another couple weeks, supposedly, before the females laid their eggs in the trees and began to kick off like the males. Mr. Biscoe lit his stainless-steel grill and a few bugs came flying out of it in flames, weaving around as if they were drunk.

"Man oh man," Crawford Tuttle said, staring at Mrs. Jennings, who was wearing sunglasses and the black leather boots. She'd shown up to the barbecue with Jules and a plate of asparagus dressed up in little scarves of meat. The meat was actually tied onto the spears. "I'd like to give her a samurai mustache."

"What the hell does that mean?" Stefano Giordano said.

Crawford shook his head. "If I have to explain it, you wouldn't understand."

"Samurais don't even have mustaches. They have goatees." Stefano turned to me, disgusted. "He makes this crap up."

I was barely listening, too distracted by Phoebe Merchant on the trampoline. She was joking around with a friend of hers, trying to double-bounce so she went extra high. She was not as beautiful as Mrs. Jennings—her mouth sloped to one side when she smiled, as if she were trying to scratch an itch on her face without touching it— but the way her hair stayed in the air after the rest of her had landed seemed like a rare and heartbreaking thing. Last night I'd had a dream about her: we were married, living in a cabin with two kids, both of whom had braces even though they were babies.

"So the latest news flash?" Stefano said, lowering his voice. "What happened to her husband? He went schizo."

"How do you know?"

"My mother told me," Stefano said. "Her cousin's friend knew him in Berkeley. They used to teach at the same college."

"But he's dead," I explained. "Jules told me himself."

Stefano shrugged. "Maybe he OD'd on his meds or something."

"I'm just glad she's unattached," Crawford said, watching Mrs. Jennings pick up one of her hors d'oeuvres. She closed her eyes and tipped her head back like a bird before taking a bite. "Jesus. I'd like to give her a Sicilian shampoo."

Jules, who'd been standing beside his mother the whole time, noticed me finally and smirked. Even though it was humid enough to leave a puddle, the freak was wearing cords again. Stefano and Crawford insisted I introduce them. The idea was that they'd cozy up to Jules and get invited to Mrs. Jennings's house, where they'd be able to impress her with their knowledge of modern art.

"How's the Cigarette Galaxy?" Crawford asked, after introducing himself. I'd told him about the poster in Jules's room.

"The what?" Jules asked.

"The Cigar Galaxy, he means," I said.

Jules glanced at me, just for a second. His mother had sauntered off with her asparagus. "I have no idea what you're talking about."

Stefano raised his eyebrows. "Do you or don't you, as Errol here claims, have a poster of the Cigarette Galaxy in your room?"

"I have a poster of Albert Einstein. Maybe he's confused." Jules looked at me curiously. "Anyway, I've never met him before in my life."

I gawked at him. "What are you talking about? You locked me in the root cellar!"

"We don't even have a root cellar."

Stefano and Crawford stared at me. I hadn't told them about the root cellar, mostly out of humiliation. Jules smiled in a new polite way and then wandered back to his mother, who was roaming the yard with her asparagus plate, as if it were not the Biscoes' party but her own. Stefano and Crawford were still looking at me, but before I could defend myself Phoebe Merchant dismounted the trampoline and landed in the grass a few yards away from us, batting furiously at her hair. I thought she was on fire. I ran to help her, prepared to tackle her on the lawn, but she'd stopped swatting her head and was staring at something in the grass.

I looked down and saw two cicadas locked together, their rear halves magically fused. One of them buzzed its wings. "What are they doing?" Phoebe Merchant asked.

I blushed. "Mating, I think."

"What do you mean?"

"I'm sorry" was all I could say. I looked at Stefano and Crawford for help, but they were standing out of earshot, their faces blank with astonishment.

"Yug," she said, shivering in disgust. "Are there more on me?"

She bent down so that her hair fell over her face. She seemed to want me to search it. I reached up and touched the sweaty roots of her hair, feeling the warmth of her scalp underneath. My heart was racing. I kept my fingers moving so she wouldn't feel them tremble.

"Nothing," I said, dropping my hands.

"No eggs or anything?"

"The female leaves the male to die," I said knowledgeably. "She lays her eggs in a tree."

"The male . . . dies?"

I nodded. Something in her voice—deliberate as a wink—made my knees catch. She thanked me for checking her hair, smiling in that lopsided way, and I realized she was trying to hide her braces. She dashed off to the cooler to grab a Sprite. I couldn't speak. The

Biscoes' lawn was green and striped like a watermelon, cluttered with sporting goods. I looked around for Jules, who'd either missed my interaction with Phoebe Merchant or was still pretending he didn't know me or anything about my tormented desire.

Eventually, dusk began to melt the windows, turning the houses into aquariums of light, and we climbed up on the Biscoes' roof with some fireworks Stefano's cousin had brought him from West Virginia. Jules seemed to be gone—or at least I'd lost sight of him. From the roof the party looked small and pointless, and I had the feeling that maybe everyone wanted to go home but were all under some kind of spell. I spied my father standing near the Biscoes' badminton net, talking to Mrs. Jennings. My mother had said goodbye to me earlier—I'd assumed for both of them—so it surprised me that he hadn't left. He was holding a badminton racket in one hand and swinging it back and forth. As he spoke, Mrs. Jennings twined one leg behind the other, stork-like, so that her feet were on opposite sides of each other. She said something and touched his arm, and my father pitched his head back and guffawed. I was astonished. I'd never seen him laugh like that before, straight into the air as if he were trying to catch his own spit.

The next evening my father pulled into the driveway after work and went straight out to the front yard to run his dogs. I watched him through the window. He always took the dogs out back, where our property sloped down to a creek, so it was odd to see Dax and Caramel pinballing around the tiny, fenced-in lawn, gobbling up bugs. My father's back was turned to the house, and when he swung around suddenly, lingering in the last bit of sun, my heart froze. He'd shaved off his beard.

When he finally came inside, my mother said theatrically, as if presenting him to us, "What do you think, boys? Does he look ten years younger?"

On the left side of his jaw was a little brown mole, as obscene to me as the beakiness of his lips. I'd seen pictures of him without a beard, prehistoric snapshots curling at the corners. Theo didn't say a word but just kept staring at his face.

"God knows what possessed him," my mother said. "I haven't seen his chin since we got married."

Her voice sounded sharper than her words, as if she were making fun of him. My father blushed. He started to say something but then stopped, thinking better of it, his nostrils hard as a statue's. He touched my head to say hello and then disappeared upstairs to his office.

The rest of the night I couldn't shake the feeling of trespassing in my own house. I lay in bed in the dark and stared at the trophies on my dresser, watching the golden swimmers strain toward me, ready to dive from their plinths. My parents argued in their bedroom. I'd heard them fight before, on rare occasions, but there was something different now about their voices, which sounded angrier the softer they got. I tried to picture Phoebe Merchant's face, the lovely way she strummed her hair to take out the tangles, as if she were playing a harp, but all I could think about was ripping her clothes off. I did my best to steer my mind back to that cabin in the woods, where our children had braces, but I couldn't stop thinking of the things I'd like to do to her. I felt tainted, polluted. My parents' voices floated down the hall. At one point I must have drifted half-asleep because I imagined that Phoebe had me in her mouth and that I looked up and saw Jules watching us from behind a tree, his creepy eye shining in the dark.

I sat up in bed. The cicadas seemed quieter than usual, and as I listened more closely their sound seemed to transform itself into *Errol Errol Errol*. I slipped on my shorts, then creaked downstairs toward the front door. The house was as still as I'd ever felt it. I unlocked the front door and stepped outside to the sidewalk. The streetlights were on, and the branches of the trees drooped with bugs, glittering where the light caught them, like clusters of stars. Above the trees the real stars shone weakly in the sky, but the constellations seemed new and unfamiliar. I could not find the Big Dipper, or Orion, or even the North Star. I'd felt real homesickness before, when my parents sent me to camp in Maine one summer, and it was a longing so bad I felt like a genie might actually appear and whisk me home again; but now I was home and felt the same ghostly longing. All around me the trees seemed alive, chanting my name and turning it strange. I checked the freckles on my arms, to reassure myself, but in the dim glow of the streetlamp they seemed less ugly, as if they'd started to fade.

The next day was so muggy no one ventured outside but kids. Crawford and Stefano stopped by in their bathing suits, but I lied about having a dentist's appointment and watched them drip off in the direction of the Giordanos' pool before heading out on my bike. I rode through the deserted neighborhood, not sure where I was going until I got there. Phoebe Merchant always practiced on the same tennis court, number 14. There was a spot on the wooded hill behind the club where Stefano and I sometimes hid inside the leafy

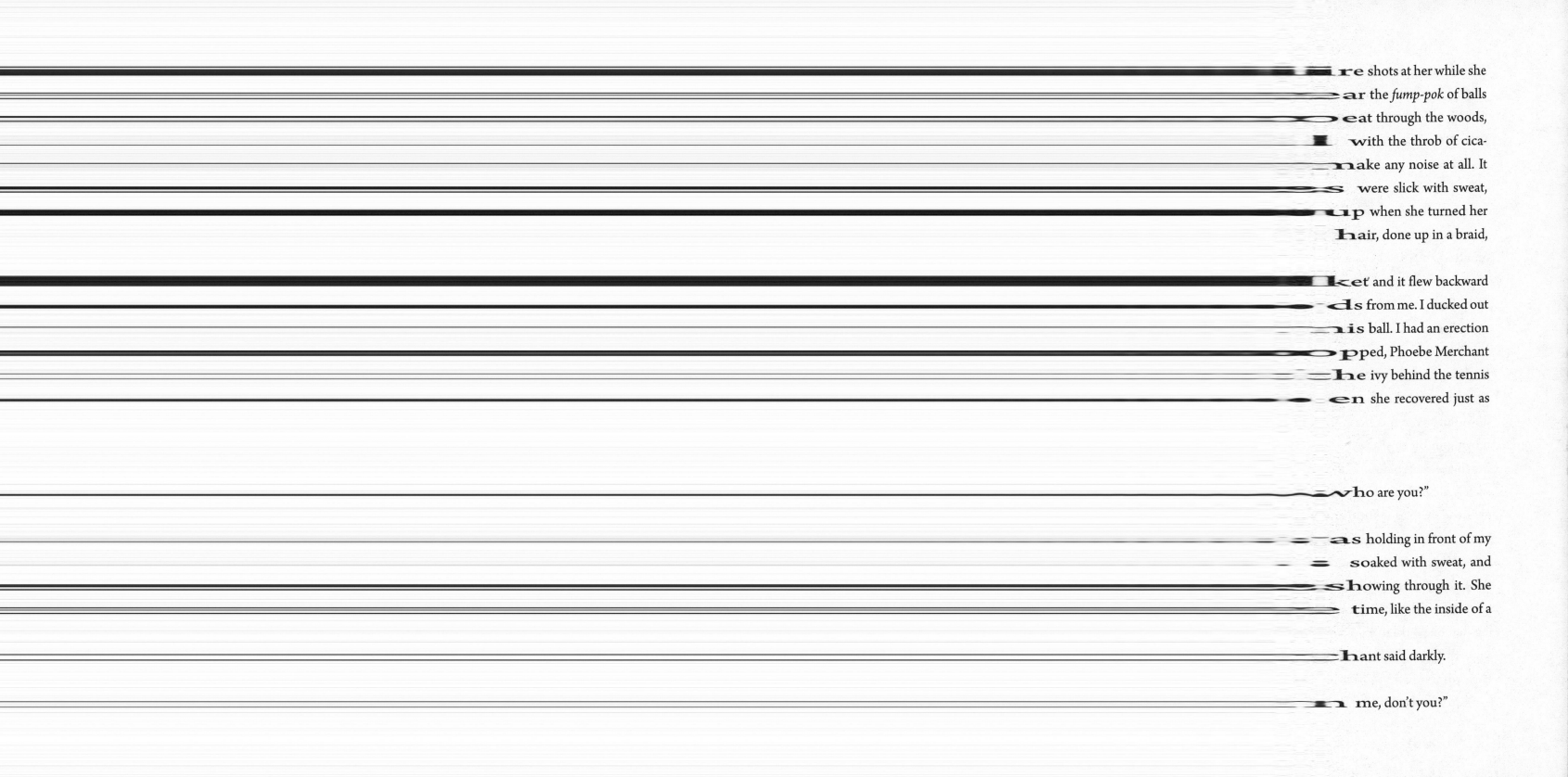

re shots at her while she

ar the *fump-pok* of balls

eat through the woods,

with the throb of cica-

make any noise at all. It

were slick with sweat,

up when she turned her

hair, done up in a braid,

ket and it flew backward

ds from me. I ducked out

is ball. I had an erection

pped, Phoebe Merchant

he ivy behind the tennis

en she recovered just as

who are you?"

as holding in front of my

soaked with sweat, and

showing through it. She

time, like the inside of a

hant said darkly.

me, don't you?"

I was too parched to speak. Sh

empty court behind her.

"I'll let you off easy this time,"

favor. "Hand me the tennis ball, an

I shook my head. This seemed

willow, a green cicada was growing

from a seed. Even its wings looke

Phoebe Merchant's face had chang

mouth. She twined one leg behin

were on the wrong sides of each ot

high above.

"I'll just have to grab it myself t

She took a step forward. My

hard-on was beating too. It didn't

Anything might happen—*was* hap

down for the tennis ball very slow

moving in outer space. She stopp

her fingers trembling. The trees scr

snatch the ball, but I dropped it an

eyes widened, as if she'd believed

hand, my heart beating against her

helped her, squeezing her more tig

through my shorts, sliding her han

myself at night. When she tore her

ing her. She'd been trying to get lo

almost tripped, breathing hard en

Her eyes were damp.

"Are you okay?"

I took a step toward her and she flinched, baring her teeth. A tiny rubber band stretched between her jaws.

I ran off and found my bike by the parking lot and steered it out to the road. The air was thick with the smell of rain. People passed me on the sidewalk but I kept my eyes on the street, imagining they'd flinch away from me the way Phoebe Merchant had. Thunder rolled in the distance. I stood up on the pedals, pumping like crazy, the bike swaying beneath me.

I got to the Jenningses' driveway and skidded to a stop. Jules was out front mowing the lawn, a sulk of boredom on his face. He wasn't wearing a shirt, and his bony back was so drenched it looked like he'd been swimming. An unlit cigarette dangled from his mouth. He reached the far end of the overgrown lawn and wheelied the mower around and shoved it into some extra-tall weeds, where it guttered to a stop.

My eyes stung. I ditched my bike and went after him. He spotted me and took off across the lawn but then lost his shoe in a pile of grass cuttings, and I tackled him near a hedge of boxwoods. "What did you do to me?" I said, straddling him.

"What are you talking about?"

"In the root cellar!"

"Nothing," Jules gasped. "I was just messing with you."

A raindrop, thick as a loogie, splashed my head. I dug my fingers into his wrists.

"How did your father die?"

"He didn't," Jules said. "He lives in Berkeley. In an apartment. With his research assistant." His eyes narrowed, and the vicious pleasure in them startled me. "Now they can fuck as much as they want."

He looked at me, his lip trembling, and the viciousness faded. Up close, his pupil looked less like a stopped clock and more like a tiny black keyhole. Strange as it sounds, this may have been the first time I really saw anyone's face. It was a young face, a scared one, and I understood why someone might want there to be more than one world. I shut my eyes for a moment.

"Boys!"

I scrambled to my feet. Mrs. Jennings stood in the doorway, wearing pajamas in the middle of the day. Her eyes were puffy, and instead of boots she had on some blue cloth slippers she must have gotten on an overseas flight. My mother had a pair just like them.

"Were you fighting?" Mrs. Jennings said.

"No," Jules said. His face was flushed.

"Let's not give them any more to gossip about. The neighbors think we're weird enough as it is."

I wondered if she was talking about my mom. It was raining now for real, stirring the cicadas into a kind of frenzy, as if they could sense that their days were numbered. I wanted, suddenly, to defend my mother.

"Will those dumb bugs ever shut up?" Mrs. Jennings said.

We were all relieved when the cicadas began to disappear. They dripped from the trees like snow and carpeted the sidewalks. Suddenly we could hear birds singing again. We could hear the scrape of our own shoes. We could hear the hum of the electrical wires festooning our street. We could hear the sprinklers chk-chk-chking on the lawns, the shrieks and splashes of swimming pools, the *kurraaang* of basketballs missing their baskets. We could hear snatches of music drifting on the breeze. We could hear the planes buzzing overhead and the bees buzzing in the flowers. We talked normally, without shouting, and our voices seemed like new and powerful instruments. For a day or two, we listened to whatever anyone had to say. My dad whispered in my mother's ear at dinner, and it was like I could hear the corny things he was saying, so badly did I want them to be true. *Out with you,* my mother said to us, giggling, *No kids allowed,* and we climbed the trees and walked barefoot in the grass, and it seemed like we might stay outside forever.

BEAUTIFUL MONSTERS

The boy is making breakfast for his sister—fried eggs and cheap frozen sausages, furred with ice—when he sees a man eating an apple from the tree outside the window. The boy drops his spatula. It is a gusty morning, sun-sharp and beautiful, and the man's shirt flags out to one side of him, rippling in the wind. The boy has never seen a grown man in real life, only in books, and the sight is both more and less frightening than he expected. The man picks another apple from high in the tree and devours it in several bites. He is bearded and tall as a shadow, but the weirdest things of all are his hands. They seem huge, grotesque, as clumsy as crabs. The veins on them bulge out, forking around his knuckles. The man plucks some more apples from the tree and sticks them in a knapsack at his feet, ducking his head so that the boy can see a saucer of scalp in the middle of his hair.

What do you think it wants? his sister whispers, joining him by the stove. She watches the hideous creature strip their tree of fruit; the boy might be out of work soon, and they need the apples themselves. The eggs have begun to scorch at the edges.

I don't know. He must have wandered away from the woods.

I thought they'd be less . . . ugly, his sister says.

The man's face is damp, streaked with ash, and it occurs to the boy that he's been crying. A twig dangles from his beard. The boy does not find the man ugly—he finds him, in fact, mesmerizing—but he does not mention this to his sister, who owns a comic book filled with pictures of handsome fathers, contraband drawings of twinkling, well-dressed men playing baseball with their daughters or throwing them high into the air. There is nothing well dressed about this man, whose filthy pants—like his shirt—look like they've been sewn from deerskin. His bare feet are black with soot. Behind him the parched mountains seethe with smoke, charred by two-week-old wildfires. There have been rumors of encounters in the woods, of firefighters beset by giant, hairy-faced beasts stealing food or tents or sleeping bags, of girls being raped in their beds.

The man stops picking apples and stares right at the kitchen window, as if he smells the eggs. The boy's heart trips. The man wipes his mouth on his sleeve, then limps down the driveway and stoops under the open door of the garage.

He's stealing something! the boy's sister says.

He barely fits, the boy says.

Trap him. We can padlock the door.

The boy goes and gets the .22 from the closet in the hall. He's never had cause to take it out before—their only intruders are skunks and possums, the occasional raccoon—but he knows exactly how to use it, a flash of certainty in his brain, just as he knows how to use the lawn mower and fix the plumbing and operate the worm-drive saw at work without thinking twice. He builds houses for other boys and girls to live in, it is what he's always done—he loves the smell of cut pine and sawdust in his nose, the *fzzzzdddt* of screws buzzing through Sheetrock into wood—and he can't imagine not doing it, any more than he can imagine leaving this windy town ringed by mountains. He was born knowing these things, will always know them; they are as instinctive to him as breathing.

But he has no knowledge of men, only what he's learned from history books. And the illicit, sentimental fairy tales of his sister's comic.

He tells his sister to stay inside and then walks toward the garage, leading with the rifle. The wind swells the trees, and the few dead August leaves crunching under his feet smell like butterscotch. For some reason, perhaps because of the sadness in the man's face, he is not as scared as he would have imagined. The boy stops inside the shadow of the garage and sees the man hunched behind the lawn mower, bent down so his head doesn't scrape the rafters. One leg of the man's pants is rolled up to reveal a bloody gash on his calf. He picks a fuel jug off the shelf and splashes some gasoline on the wound, grimacing. The boy clears his throat, loudly, but the man doesn't look up.

Get out of my garage, the boy says.

The man startles, banging his head on the rafters. He grabs a shovel leaning against the wall and holds it in front of him. The shovel, in his overgrown hands, looks as small as a baseball bat. The boy lifts the .22 up to his eye, so that it's leveled at the man's stomach. He tilts the barrel at the man's face.

What will you do?

Shoot you, the boy says.

The man smiles, dimpling his filthy cheeks. His teeth are as yellow as corn. I'd like to see you try.

I'd aim right for the apricot. The medulla. You'd die instantly.

You look like you're nine, the man mutters.

The boy doesn't respond to this. He suspects the man's disease has infected his brain. Slowly, the man puts down the shovel and ducks out of the garage, plucking cobwebs from his face. In the sunlight, the wound on his leg looks even worse, shreds of skin stuck to it like grass. He reeks of gasoline and smoke and something else, a foul body smell, like the inside of a ski boot.

I was sterilizing my leg.

Where do you live? the boy asks.

In the mountains. The man looks at his gun. Don't worry, I'm by myself. We split up so we'd be harder to kill.

Why?

Things are easier to hunt in a herd.

No, the boy says. Why did you leave?

The fire. Burned up everything we were storing for winter. The man squints at the house. Can I trouble you for a spot of water?

The boy lowers his gun, taking pity on this towering creature that seems to have stepped out of one of his dreams. In the dreams, the men are like beautiful monsters, stickered all over with leaves, roaming through town in the middle of the night. The boy leads the man inside the house, where his sister is still standing at the window. The man looks at her and nods. That someone should have hair growing out of his face appalls her even more than the smell. *There's a grown man in my house,* she says to herself, but she cannot reconcile the image this arouses in her brain with the stooped creature she sees limping into the kitchen. She's often imagined what it would be like to live with a father—a dashing giant, someone who'd buy her presents and whisk her chivalrously from danger, like the brave, mortal fathers she reads about—but this man is as far from a handsome creature as can be.

And yet the sight of his sunburned hands, big enough to snap her neck, stirs something inside her, an unreachable itch.

They have no chairs large enough for him, so the boy puts two side by side. He goes to the sink and returns with a mug of water. The man drinks the water in a single gulp, then immediately asks for another.

How old are you? the girl says suspiciously.

The man picks the twig from his beard. Forty-six.

The girl snorts.

No, really. I'm aging by the second.

The girl blinks, amazed. She's lived for thirty years and can't imagine what it would be like for her body to mark the time. The man lays the twig on the table, ogling the cantaloupe sitting on the counter. The boy unsheathes a cleaver from the knife block and slices the melon in two, spooning out the pulp before chopping off a generous piece. He puts the orange smile of melon on a plate. The man devours it without a spoon, holding it like a harmonica.

Where do you work? the man asks suddenly, gazing out the window at the pickup in the driveway. The toolbox in the bed glitters in the sun.

Out by Old Harmony, the boy says. We're building some houses.

Anything to put your brilliant skills to use, eh?

Actually, we're almost finished, the boy says. The girl looks at him: increasingly, the boy and girl are worried about the future. The town has reached its population cap, and rumor is there are no plans to raise it again.

Don't worry, the man says, sighing. They'll just repurpose you. Presto chango.

How do *you* know? the girl asks.

I know about Perennials. You think I'm an ignorant ape? The man shakes his head. Jesus. The things I could teach you in my sleep.

The girl smirks. Like what?

The man opens his mouth as if to speak but then closes it again, staring at the pans hanging over the stove. They're arranged, like the tailbones of a dinosaur, from large to small. His face seems to droop. I bet you, um, can't make the sound of a loon.

What?

With your hands and mouth? A loon call?

The boy feels nothing in his brain: an exotic blankness. The feeling frightens him. The man perks up, seeming to recover his spirits. He cups his hands together as if warming them and blows into his thumbs, fluttering one hand like a wing. The noise is perfect and uncanny: the ghostly call of a loon.

The girl grabs the cleaver from the counter. How did you do that?

Ha! Experts of the universe! The man smiles, eyes bright with disdain. Come here and I'll teach you.

The girl refuses, still brandishing the knife, but the boy swallows his fear and approaches the table. The man shows him how to cup his hands together in a box and then tells him to blow into his knuckles. The boy tries, but no sound comes out. The man laughs. The boy blows until his cheeks hurt, until he's ready to give up, angry at the whole idea of birdcalls and at loons for making them, which only makes the man laugh harder. He pinches the boy's thumbs together. The boy recoils, so rough and startling is the man's touch. Trembling, the boy presses his lips to his knuckles again and blows, producing a low airy whistle that surprises him—his chest filling with something he can't explain, a shy arrogant pleasure, like a blush.

The boy and girl let the man use their shower. While he's undressing, they creep outside and take turns at the bathroom window, their hands cupped to the glass, sneaking looks at his strange hairy body and giant shoulders tucked in like a vulture's and long terrible penis, which shocks them when he turns. The girl is especially shocked by the scrotum. It's limp and bushy and speckled with veiny bursts. She has read about the ancient way of making babies, has even tried to imagine what it would be like to grow a fetus in her belly, a tiny bean-size thing blooming into something curled and sac-bound and miraculous. She works as an assistant in a lab where embryos are grown, and she wonders sometimes, staring at the tanks of black-eyed little beings, all the brothers and sisters farmed from frozen eggs, what it would be like to raise one of them and smoosh him to her breast, like a gorilla mother does. Sometimes she even feels a pang of loneliness when they're hatched, encoded with all the knowledge they'll ever need, sent off to the orphanage to be raised until they're old enough for treatments. But, of course, the same thing happened to her, and what does she have to feel lonely about?

Once in a while the girl will peek into her brother's room and see him getting dressed for work, see his little bobbing string of a penis, vestigial as his appendix, and her mouth will dry up. It lasts only for a second, this feeling, before her brain commands it to stop.

Now, staring at the man's hideous body, she feels her mouth dry up in the same way, aware of each silent bump of her heart.

The man spends the night. A fugitive, the boy calls him, closing the curtains so that no one can see in. The man's clothes are torn and stiff with blood, stinking of secret man-things, so the boy gives him his bathrobe to wear as a T-shirt and fashions a pair of shorts out of some sweatpants, slitting the elastic so that they fit his waist. The man changes into his new clothes, exposing the little beards under his arms. He seems happy with his ridiculous outfit and even does a funny bow that makes the boy laugh. He tries it on the girl as well, rolling his hand through the air in front of him, but she scowls and shuts the door to her room.

As the week stretches on, the girl grows more and more unhappy. There's the smell of him every morning, a sour blend of sweat and old-person breath and nightly blood seeping into the gauze the boy uses to dress his wound. There's his ugly limp, the hockey stick he's taken to using as a cane and which you can hear clopping from every room of the house. There's the cosmic stench he leaves in the bathroom, so powerful it makes her eyes water. There are the paper airplanes littering the backyard, ones he's taught the boy to make, sleek and bird-nosed and complicated as origami. Normally, the boy and girl drink a beer together in the kitchen after work—sometimes he massages her feet while they listen to music—but all week when she gets home he's out back with the man, flying his stupid airplanes around the yard. He checks the man's face after every throw, which makes her feel like going outside with a flyswatter and batting the planes down. The yard is protected by a windbreak of pines, but the girl worries one of the neighbors might see somehow and call the police. If anyone finds out there's a man in their house, she could get fired from the lab. They might even put her in jail.

Sometimes the man yells at them. The outbursts are unpredict-able. *Turn that awful noise down!* he'll yell if they're playing music while he's trying to watch the news. Once, when the girl answers her phone during dinner, the man grabs it from her hand and hurls it into the sink. Next time, he tells her, he'll smash it with a brick. The worst thing is that they have to do what he says to quiet him down.

If it comes to it, she will kill the man. She will grab the .22 and shoot him while he sleeps.

On Saturday, the girl comes back from the grocery store and the man is limping around the backyard with the boy on his shoulders. The lawn mower sits in a spiral of mown grass. The boy laughs, and she hisses at them that the neighbors will hear. The man plunks the boy down and then sweeps her up and heaves her onto his shoulders instead. The girl is taller than she's ever imagined, so tall that she can see into the windows of her upstairs room. The mulchy smell of grass fills her nose. She wraps her legs around the man's neck. A shiver goes through her, as if she's climbed out of a lake. The shiver doesn't end so much as work its way inside of her, as elusive as a hair in her throat. The man trots around the yard and she can't help herself, she begins to laugh as the boy did, closing her legs more tightly around his neck, giggling in a way she's never giggled before—a weird, high-pitched sound, as if she can't control her own mouth—ducking under the lowest branches of the pin oak shading the back porch. The man starts to laugh too. Then he sets her down and falls to all fours on the lawn and the boy climbs on top of him, spurring him with his heels, and the man tries in vain to buck him off, whinnying like a horse in the fresh-mown grass. The boy clutches the man's homemade shirt. The girl watches them ride around the yard for a minute, the man's face bright with joy, their long shadow bucking like a single creature, and then she comes up from behind and pushes the boy off, so hard it knocks the wind out of him.

The boy squints at the girl, whose face has turned red. She has never pushed him for any reason. The boy stares at her face, so small and smooth and freckled compared to the man's, and for the first time is filled with disgust.

The man hobbles to his feet, gritting his teeth. His leg is bleeding. The gauze is soaked, a dark splotch of blood leaking spidery trickles down his shin.

Look what you've done! the boy says before helping the man to the house.

That night, the girl starts from a dream, as if her spine has been plucked. The man is standing in the corner of her room, clutching the hockey stick. His face—hideous, weirdly agleam—floats in the moonlight coming through the window. Her heart begins to race. She wonders if he's come to rape her. The man wipes his eyes with the end of his robe, first one, then the other. Then he clops toward her and sits on the edge of the bed, so close she can smell the sourness of his breath. His eyes are still damp. I was just watching you sleep, he says. He begins to sing to her, the same sad song he croons in the shower, the one about traveling through this world of woe. *There's no sickness, toil, or danger, in that bright land to which I go.* While he sings, he strokes the girl's hair with the backs of his fingers, tucking some loose strands behind her ear. His knuckles, huge and scratchy, feel like acorns.

What's the bright land? the girl asks.

The man stops stroking her hair. Heaven, he says.

The girl has heard about these old beliefs; to think that you could live on after death is so quaint and gullible, it touches her strangely.

Did someone you know die?

The man doesn't answer her. She can smell the murk of his sweat. Trembling, the girl reaches out and touches his knee where the sweatpants end, feeling its wilderness of hair. She moves her fingers under the hem of his sweats. The man does not move, closing his eyes as she inches her fingers up his leg. His breathing coarsens. Outside the wind picks up and rattles the window screen. Very suddenly, the man recoils, limping up from the bed.

You're just a girl, he whispers.

She stares at him. His face is turned, as if he can't bear to look at her. She does not know what she is.

He calls her Sleepyhead and hobbles out of the room. She wonders at this strange name for her, so clearly an insult. Her eyes burn. Outside her window the moon looks big and stupid, a sleeping head.

The next day, when the boy comes home from work, the house is humid with the smell of cooking. The man is bent over the stove, leaning to one side to avoid putting too much weight on his injured leg. It's been over a week now and the gash doesn't look any better; in fact, the smell has started to change, an almondy stink like something left out in the rain. Yesterday, when the boy changed the bandage, the skin underneath the pus was yellowish brown, the color of an old leaf. But the boy's not worried. He's begun to see the man as some kind of god. All day long he looks forward to driving home from work and finding this huge ducking presence in his house, smelling the day's sweat of his body through his robe. He feels a helpless urge to run to him. The man always seems slightly amazed to see him, perturbed even, but in a grateful way, shaking his head as if he's spotted something he thought he'd lost, and though the boy can't articulate his feelings to himself, it's this amazement that he's been waiting for and that fills him with such restlessness at work. Ahoy there, the man says. It's not particularly funny, even kind of stupid, but the boy likes it. Ahoy, he says back. Sometimes the man clutches the boy's shoulder while he changes his bandage, squeezing so hard the boy can feel it like a live wire up his neck, and the boy looks forward to this, too, even though it hurts them both.

Now the man lifts the frying pan from the stove and serves the boy and girl dinner. The boy looks at his plate: a scrawny-looking thing with the fur skinned off, like a miniature greyhound fried to a crisp. A squirrel.

I caught them in the backyard, the man explains.

Disgusting! the girl says, making a face.

Would you rather go to your room, young lady? the man says.

She pushes her chair back.

No, please. I'm sorry. You don't have to eat. He looks at his plate and frowns. My mother was the real cook. She could have turned this into a fricassee.

What are they like? the boy asks.

What?

Mothers.

They're wonderful, the man says after a minute. Though some-times you hate them. You hate them for years and years.

Why?

That's a good question. The man cuts off a piece of squirrel but instead of eating it stares at the window curtain, still bright with day-light at six o'clock. I remember when I was a kid, how hard it was to go to sleep in the summer. I used to tell my mom to turn off the day. That's what I'd say, *Turn off the day,* and she'd reach up and pretend to turn it off.

The man lifts his hand and yanks at the air, as if switching off a light.

The boy eats half his squirrel even though it tastes a little bit like turpentine. He wants to make the man happy. He knows that the man is sad, and that it has to do with something that happened in the woods. The man has told him about the town where he grew up, nestled in the mountains many miles away—the last colony of its kind—and how some boys and girls moved in eventually and forced everyone out of their homes. How they spent years traveling around, searching for a spot where there was enough wilderness to hide in so they wouldn't be discovered, where the food and water were plentiful, eventually settling in the parklands near the boy and girl's house. But the boy's favorite part is hearing about the disease itself: how exciting it was for the man to watch himself change, to grow tall and hairy and dark-headed, as strong as a beast. To feel ugly sometimes and hear his voice deepen into a stranger's. To fall in love with a woman's body and watch a baby come out of her stomach, still tied to her by a rope of flesh. The boy loves this part most of all, but when he asks about it, the man grows quiet and then says he understands why Perennials want to live forever. Did you have a baby like that? the boy asked him yesterday, and the man got up and limped into the backyard and stayed there for a while, picking up some stray airplanes and crumpling them into balls.

After dinner, they go into the living room to escape the lingering smell of squirrel. Sighing, the man walks to the picture window and opens up the curtains and looks out at the empty street. Bats flicker under the streetlamps. He's told them that when he was young the streets were filled with children: they played until it was dark, building things or shooting each other with sticks or playing Butts Up and Capture the Flag and Ghost in the Graveyard, games that he's never explained.

It's a beautiful evening, he says, sighing again.

The girl does not look up from her pocket computer, her eyes burning as they did last night. Just listening to him talk about how nice it is outside, like he knows what's best for them, makes her clench her teeth.

What did you do when it rained? the boy asks.

Puppet shows, the man says, brightening.

Puppet shows?

The man frowns. Performances! For our mom and dad. My brother and I would write our own scripts and memorize them. The man glances at the girl on the floor, busy on her computer. He claps in her face, loudly, but she doesn't look up. Can you get me a marker and some different-colored socks?

They won't fit you, the boy says.

We'll do a puppet show. The three of us.

The boy grins. What about?

Anything. Pretend you're kids like I was.

We'll do one for *you,* the boy says, sensing how much this would please the man.

He goes to get some socks from his room and then watches as the man draws eyes and a nose on each one. The girl watches too, avoiding the man's face. If it will make the boy happy, she will do what he wants. They disappear into the boy's room to think up a script. After a while, they come out with the puppets on their hands and crouch behind the sofa, as the man's instructed them. The puppet show begins.

Hello, red puppet.

Hello, white puppet.

I can't even drive.

Me either.

Let's play Capture the Graveyard.

Okay.

In seventy years I'm going to die. First, though, I will grow old and weak and disease-ridden. This is called aging. It was thought to be incurable, in the Age of Senescence.

Will you lose your hair?

I am male, so there's a four in seven chance of baldness.

If you procreate with me, my breasts will become engorged with milk.

I'm sorry.

Don't apologize. The milk will feed my baby.

But how?

It will leak from my nipples.

I do not find you disgusting, red puppet. Many animals have milk-producing mammary glands. I just wish it wasn't so expensive to grow old and die.

Everyone will have to pay more taxes, because we'll be too feeble to work and pay for our useless medicines.

Jesus Christ, the man says, interrupting them. He limps over and yanks the socks from their hands. What's wrong with you?

Nothing, the girl says.

Can't you even do a fucking puppet show?

He limps into the boy's room and shuts the door. The boy does not know what he's done to make him angry. Bizarrely, he feels like he might cry. He sits on the couch for a long time, staring out the window at the empty street. Moths eddy under the streetlamps like snow. The girl is jealous of his silence; she has never made the boy look like this, as if he might throw up from unhappiness. She walks to the window and shuts the curtains without speaking and shows him something on her computer: a news article, all about the tribe of Senescents. There have been twelve sightings in three days. Most have managed to elude capture, but one, a woman, was shot by a policeboy as she tried to climb through his neighbor's window. There's a close-up of her body, older even than the man's, her face gruesome with wrinkles. A detective holds her lips apart with two fingers to reveal the scant yellow teeth, as crooked as fence posts. The girl calls up another picture: a crowd of children, a search party, many of them holding rifles. They are standing in someone's yard, next to a garden looted of vegetables. The town is offering an official reward for any Senescent captured. Five thousand dollars, dead or alive. The girl widens her eyes, hoping the boy will widen his back, but he squints at her as if he doesn't know who she is.

*   *   *

At work, the boy has fallen behind on the house he's drywalling. The tapers have already begun on the walls downstairs. In the summer heat, the boy hangs the last panel of Sheetrock upstairs and then sits down to rest in the haze of gypsum dust. He has always liked this chalky smell, always felt that his work meant something: he was building homes for new Perennials to move into and begin their lives. But something has changed. The boy looks through the empty window square beside him and sees the evergreens that border the lot. Before long they'll turn white with snow and then drip themselves dry and then go back to being as green and silent and lonely-looking as they are now. It will happen, the boy thinks, in the blink of an eye.

There's a utility knife sitting by his boot, and he picks it up and imagines what it would be like to slit his throat.

Did you see the news this morning? his coworker, a taper who was perennialized so long ago he's stopped counting the years, asks at lunch.

The boy shakes his head, struggling to keep his eyes open. He has not been sleeping well on the couch.

They found another Senescent, at the hospital. He wanted shots.

But it's too late, the boy says. Their cells are corrupted.

Apparently the dumb ape didn't know that. The police promised to treat him if he told them where the new camp is.

The boy's scalp tightens. What camp?

Where most of them ended up 'cause of the fire.

Did he tell them?

Conover Pass, the taper says, laughing. I wouldn't be surprised if there's a mob on its way already.

The boy drives home after work, his eyes so heavy he can barely focus on the road. Conover Pass is not far from his house; he would have taken the man there, perhaps, if he'd known. It's been a month since the boy first saw him in the yard, devouring apples, so tall and mighty that he seemed invincible. Now the man can barely finish a piece of toast. The boy changes his bandages every night, without being asked, though secretly he's begun to dread it. The wound is beginning to turn black and fungal. It smells horrible, like a dead possum. When the man needs a bath, the boy has to undress him, gripping his waist to help him into the tub. His arms are thinner than the boy's, angular as wings, and his penis floating in the bath looks shriveled and weed-like. The boy leaves the bathroom, embarrassed. It's amazing to think that this frail, bony creature ever filled him with awe.

Last night the man asked the boy to put his dead body under the ground. Don't let them take it away, he said.

Shhhh, the boy said, tucking a pillow under the man's head.

I don't want to end up in a museum or something.

You're not going to die, the boy said stupidly. He blushed, wondering why he felt compelled to lie. Perhaps this was what being a Senescent was like. You had to lie all the time, convincing yourself that you weren't going to disappear. He said it again, more vehemently, and saw a gleam of hope flicker in the man's eye.

Ahoy there, the man says now when he gets home.

Ahoy.

The smell is worse than usual. The man has soiled his sheets. The boy helps him from bed and lets him lean his weight on one shoulder and then walks him to the bathtub, where he cleans him off with a washcloth. The blackness has spread down to his foot; the leg looks like a rotting log. The boy has things to do—it's his turn to cook dinner, and there's a stack of bills that need to go out tomorrow—and now he has to run laundry on top of everything else. He grabs the man's wrists and tries to lift him out of the bathtub, but his arms are like dead things. The man won't flex them enough to be useful. The boy kneels and tries to get him out by his armpits, but the man slips from his hands and crashes back into the tub. He howls in pain, cursing the boy.

The boy leaves him in the tub and goes into the kitchen, where the girl is washing dishes from breakfast. The bills on the table have not been touched.

He'll be dead in a week, the girl says.

The boy doesn't respond.

I did some math this morning. We've got about three months, after you're furloughed.

The boy looks at her. The man has become a burden to him as well—she can see this in his face. She can see, too, that he loves this pathetic creature that came into their life to die, though she knows just as certainly that he'll be relieved once it happens. He might not admit it, but he will be.

I'll take care of us, the girl says tenderly.

How?

She looks down at the counter. Go distract him.

The boy does not ask why. The man will die, but he and the girl will be together forever. He goes back into the bathroom; the man has managed to get out of the tub but has fallen onto the floor. He is whimpering. The boy slides an arm around his waist and helps him back to bed. A lightning bug has gotten through the window, strobing very slowly around the room, but the man doesn't seem to notice.

What do you think about when you're old? the boy asks.

The man laughs. Home, I guess.

Do you mean the woods?

Childhood, he says, as if it were a place.

So you miss it, the boy says after a minute.

When you're a child, you can't wait to get out. Sometimes it's hell.

Through the wall, the boy hears his sister on the phone: the careful, well-dressed voice she uses with strangers. He feels sick.

At least there's heaven, he says, trying to console the man.

The man looks at him oddly, then frowns. Where I can be like you?

A tiny feather, small as a snowflake, clings to the man's eyelash. The boy does something strange. He wets his finger in the glass on the bedside table and traces a T on the man's forehead. He has no idea what this means; it's half-remembered trivia. The man tries to smile. He reaches up and yanks the air.

The man closes his eyes; it takes the boy a moment to realize he's fallen asleep. The flares of the lightning bug are brighter now. Some water trickles from the man's forehead and drips down his withered face. The boy tries to remember what it was like to see it for the first time—chewing on an apple, covered in ash—but the image has already faded to a blur, distant as a dream.

He listens for sirens. The screech of tires. Except for the chirring of crickets, the evening is silent.

The boy feels suddenly trapped, frightened, as if he can't breathe.

He walks into the living room, but it doesn't help. The hallway, too, oppresses him. It's like being imprisoned in his own skin. His heart beats inside his neck, strong and steady. Beats and beats and beats. Through the skylight in the hall, he can see the first stars beginning to glimmer out of the dusk. They will go out eventually, shrinking into nothing. When he lifts the .22 from the closet, his hands—so small and tame and birdlike—feel unbearably captive.

He does not think about what he's doing, or whether there's time or not to do it—only that he will give the man what he wants: bury his body in the ground, like a treasure.

He walks back into the bedroom with the gun. The man is sleeping quietly, his breathing quick and shallow. His robe sags open to reveal a pale triangle of chest, bony as a fossil. The boy tries to imagine what it would be like to be on earth for such a short time. Forty-six years. It would be like you never even lived. He can actually see the man's skin moving with his heart, fluttering up and down. The boy aims the gun at this mysterious failing thing.

He touches the trigger, dampening it with sweat, but can't bring himself to squeeze it. He cannot kill this doomed and sickly creature. Helplessly, he imagines the policeboys carrying the man away, imagines the look on the man's face as he realizes what the boy has done. His eyes hard with blame. But no: the man wouldn't know he had anything to do with it. He won't get in trouble.

The boy and girl will go back to their old lives again. No one to grumble at them or cook them dinners they don't want or make him want to cry.

The boy's relief gives way to a ghastly feeling in his chest, as if he's done something terrible.

Voices echo from the street outside. The boy rushes to the window and pulls back the curtains. A mob of boys and girls yelling in the dusk, parading from the direction of Conover Pass, holding poles with human heads on top of them. The skewered heads bob through the air like puppets. *Off to bed without your supper!* one of the boys says in a gruff voice, something he's read in a book, and the others copy him—*Off to bed! Off to bed!*—pretending to be grown-ups. The heads gawk at each other from their poles. They look startled to the boy, still surprised by their betrayal. One turns in the boy's direction, haloed by flies, and for a moment its eyes seem to get even bigger, as though it's seen a monster. Then it spins away to face the others. Freed from their bodies, nimble as children, the heads dance down the street.

MOTHERSHIP

Just as Jess was getting out of Clayton House treatment center, her brother-in-law got a brain tumor. Typical, to be upstaged by a brain tumor. She'd tried to kill herself, then burned through her inheritance in order to spend six months doing group therapy with crazy people, but all her sister could talk about was the lump in her husband's brain. They were sitting in the lobby of Cedars-Sinai while Frank rested in his room upstairs. The place had climate-controlled itself back to the Ice Age, but Margot was wearing a gauzy tunic thing and shorts. Men in scrubs—doctors—stared at her as they walked by. Jess, who'd watched men ogle her sister's tits since she was about fourteen, felt like a gargoyle.

It wasn't even a real tumor. It was a benign one, but something wonky had happened during the surgery and Frank couldn't feel half his body. That's what the surgeon had said: "wonky." Margot could not get over this.

"This is Los Angeles. Who says 'wonky'?"

"He means they fucked up," Jess said.

"Shhh," Margot said, before mocking herself: *"There are children present."*

Jess's nephew roared like a saber-tooth, practicing for Halloween. Jess had never appreciated what it meant to have children present until she'd spent two days sleeping in her sister's house, a beautiful Mediterranean that—despite its estimated market value—was about as roomy as a houseboat. Every morning at 6:15, her niece and nephew barged into the living room and began jumping on the sofa bed as if it were a trampoline. Never mind that Jess's arms and legs and ovaries were hidden under the sheets. Motion-sick, mummified inside a trazodone hangover, she had to keep herself from cursing at them. "Your father has a brain tumor!" she scolded them once, forgetting that she'd flown down from Portland to help out.

Other than that—like the rest of Margot's accomplishments— the children were perfect. Strangers gasped when they saw those beach-bronzed faces, actually threw their hands over their hearts. Floyd, despite his Faulknerian name, was the four-year-old boy every progressive couple dreams about. He worshipped trucks and yet never bit or punched or threw his food on the floor. His favorite color, inevitably, was pink. Ellory was seven years old and had already read the entire Harry Potter series to herself several times over. She ate sushi and Brussels sprouts. Of course, she was *bored to death* at school.

"You're scaring me, Mr. F," Jess said now, responding to Floyd's roars. She'd heard Margot call him "Mr. F" last night. That was her strategy: to impersonate Margot as much as possible, thereby transforming herself into a decent aunt. "I didn't know saber-toothed tigers were so vicious."

"Actually, it's saber-toothed *cat*," Ellory said offhandedly. "They're not technically part of the tiger family."

"That can't be true," Jess said. "We always called it 'tiger.'"

"Lots of people make that mistake. It's a missed conception."

"She's right, I'm afraid," Margot said, smiling at her daughter.

Jess felt something curdle in her throat. She did not feel good about this, disliking her own niece, but certain things were beyond one's power. Yesterday, Ellory had shown Jess how to use an iPad, soothing her when she got frustrated. "We learned Technology in first grade," she'd actually said.

Now Floyd asked for the tenth time about the "hotel" she'd been living in. Jess had made the mistake of calling it that—a hotel—the first day she arrived, not realizing he was a fan of the Eloise books. "My roommate liked to cook rocks," she said, trying to disabuse him of the idea. "She'd collect them from outside and then fry them up in a pan—or pretend to."

"Why?" Floyd asked.

Jess shrugged. The roommate, an obese schizophrenic woman, had never felt the need to explain herself. "You know how some people are born to be whatever? Basketball players? She was born to cook rocks."

"Are you sure you want to be telling them this?" Margot said, taking off the velvet fedora she'd been wearing all morning. She had become one of those hip moms that dressed like Stevie Nicks, invincible in sunglasses. She was eighteen months older than Jess, had breast-fed her children until they were two, but looked five years younger.

"People aren't born to do anything," Ellory insisted.

"Oh?"

"They make their own destiny. Like Harry Potter."

Jess frowned, staring at the buckteeth that mysteriously—*providentially*—made her niece even more beautiful. Beyond Ellory, sitting in the middle of the lobby, was the Claes Oldenburg sculpture of a giant ice bag; Floyd pressed a button and the hideous sculpture began to inflate like a balloon. Jess did not like hospitals—in fact, they made her soul retch—though this one bore about as much resemblance to Emanuel Medical Center, where she'd had her stomach pumped, as the Taj Mahal. How much the kids knew about her suicide attempt, Jess wasn't sure. Margot had promised to stick to the official line, that Jess had decided to move sunward, fed up with the soggy winters of Portland, and was staying with them for a couple of weeks while she decided what to do next. And the truth was, Margot needed her, seeing as she was spending half her days at the rehab unit with Frank: amazing how much time and energy and mileage two children could burn through. Probably not her first choice of nannies, their suicidal aunt, but Frank's mother had already been out for a week. (Their own mother, who'd done enough damage the first time around, was not an option.)

"Sure you're up to it?" Margot said, handing over her car keys. "Taking them trick-or-treating?"

Jess nodded. She'd agreed to escort the kids around while Margot stayed at the hospital—Frank had an MRI scheduled at 5:00—but now she wondered if it was such a good idea. The ice bag was deflating, making a ghastly robotic noise. Margot kissed Floyd goodbye and then crouched down to her daughter's height. She put her face to Ellory's face, and they closed their eyes, rubbing their noses back and forth as if snuffing out an itch. "Nunka nunka," Ellory said, leaning her forehead against her mother's. It was an extraordinary farewell, the best case for human reproduction Jess had seen in a long time.

"Don't forget about Floyd," her sister said. "No Snickers or anything with peanuts."

"My face explodes," Floyd said.

"Blows up," Ellory corrected him.

"I could stop breathing," Floyd said happily. He began to dance around the lobby, gyrating his pelvis. "Everybody knows I'm a motherfuckin' monster," he sang.

Margot straightened. "Where did you learn that?"

Ellory, the little narc, looked at Jess. She'd played the CD in the car yesterday, driving the kids to the science museum. Jess hadn't even thought about the lyrics, or the fact that she was singing along, till Ellory had asked her what the N-word meant.

Margot turned to Jess, her eyes hooded with exhaustion, and for the first time Jess fully considered how much stress she was under. Her sister shook her head, more in amazement than in reproach. "What's wrong with you?"

Jess looked at the floor, feeling the old ripple of self-loathing. It was the question of her life. Some people's question was *Can you design the perfect toothbrush?* or *Are you willing to cross the Sonoran Desert for the chance at a better life?* Hers was *What the fuck is wrong with you?* It hadn't always been like this, of course, at least not when they were girls—there had been a time when Margot seemed proud to have her for a sister, bragging to her friends about how smart Jess was. What delirious joy she'd felt hearing this. Or riding in the backseat with Margot on vacations, the two of them making up songs about imaginary diseases. (*Oh, try not to catch noselitis from a raven, or your nose will energetically cave in!*) Sometimes, even now, Jess would catch a glimpse of Margot when she wasn't looking and her heart would gust toward her sister, nimble as a kite. Jess could almost forget about the countless ways she'd fucked up, like failing to make it to Margot's wedding. But then Margot would catch her eye and her face would frown without meaning to—from concern or disappointment, it was hard to say.

Still, Jess was here now. Lending a hand. It was not too late to win Margot back. All she needed was to prove she was well, or at least well medicated: a good aunt, who keeps her motherfucking desperation to herself. The first step was to get Ellory to like her.

Jess loaded Floyd into his car seat while Ellory struggled with her seat belt. In her care, Margot's VW had begun to smell like a dumpster; the brown toadstool of an apple core stood on the backseat. Jess walked to Ellory's side and leaned over her lap to snap her seat belt, obscurely touched by the girl's inability to do it herself. She put her face to Ellory's so that they were nose to nose, stilling her niece's head with two hands. "Nunka nunka," she said. For a moment, as Ellory began to kiss her nose with her own, Jess felt a tenderness that stole her breath. A sliver of Margot's happiness. Ellory's hair smelled clovey and warm, like her mother's. But then Jess realized her niece had gone stiff: the girl wasn't rubbing noses with her at all, but shaking her head no.

One of Jess's earliest memories was getting her face painted at the street fair—"Princess Beauty," she'd asked for—and then bursting into tears when she looked nothing like Margot. For Jess, this was the first of many disappointments, paving the way for a remarkable streak of adult failures. There was her crack at rock 'n' roll stardom, starving to death in Queens while her bandmates—friends from college—grew increasingly fed up with poverty. There was Teach for America and the swift realization that she did not want to do anything for America, particularly if it meant living in West Texas and being a babysitter. There was the aborted PhD in English, the less said the better. There was the long string of restaurant jobs, in New York and Providence and Portland, finally derailed by her inability to work from bed.

Jess had suffered bouts of "depression" in college, of course, like everyone else: days spent moping around her room, sick with the futility of it all, breaking into tears when a lightbulb burned out and she had to change it. But this was different. Nothing in life—or in literature, for that matter, or art or cinema or philosophy—had prepared her for it. It was not nausea, or fear and trembling, or a scream on a bridge. It was not a black dog. It was not a fucking bell jar. It was not chatting with a skull, or throwing your arms around a flogged horse, or walking back to the hotel in the rain.

This is what it was: a Shrinky Dink. Getting shut up in an oven and curling up slowly and then finally shrinking into a Dink, a dead useless thing that's no longer you. The Dink can barely think. It can barely move or talk. It definitely cannot cook. For the Dink Formerly Known as Jess, this meant eating miso soup powder straight from the packet, like Fun Dip. It meant not changing the kitty litter for a month, until her bed was filled with cat shit and putrid muddy clumps. It meant smelling so bad that a manager at Trader Joe's tried to give her an apple. It meant never answering the phone or returning messages. It meant that her family and her friends and everyone she'd ever cared about over the strange and unrepeatable thirty-five years she'd been on earth made her sick. It meant lying in bed until time lost its meaning and she was floating through the cosmos, threading the universe back into itself, past the Big Bang into the No Bang, the Big Fat Nothing, and then checking the clock to see that six hours had passed and she was still lying in the same place, in her bed of shit, Napoleon meowing beside her. It meant leaving the front door open on purpose so that the miserable cat might disappear, then not feeling anything when he did. It meant thinking about slicing her own throat—not once or twice a day, but obsessively, *affectionately*, picturing the blade going through the skin, blood spraying from her neck. It meant knowing that nothing would make the slightest bit of difference to her or bring her even a nanosecond of joy. The Nobel Peace Prize, a million dollars, a life like Margot's—a genie could offer them to her, right then and there, and she wouldn't bother to get out of bed and accept them.

By the end, it was like having a string attached to your brain. You pulled the string and it said: *I wish you hadn't pulled that.*

I wish you hadn't pulled that. I wish you hadn't pulled that. I wish you hadn't pulled that. I wish you hadn't pulled that. I wish you hadn't pulled that. I wish you hadn't pulled that. I wish you hadn't pulled that. I wish you hadn't pulled that. I wish you hadn't pulled that. I wish you hadn't pulled that. I wish you hadn't pulled that. I wish you hadn't pulled that. I wish you hadn't pulled that. I wish you hadn't pulled that. I wish you hadn't pulled that.

Now, getting ready to take Floyd and Ellory trick-or-treating, Jess tried not to think about thinking. It was a slippery slope, and at the bottom was the word "slippery," waiting for her like a banana peel. She stared at the wedding picture above the TV: Margot's head thrown back in laughter, Frank looking at her adoringly, a glass of champagne in his hand. Jess had always had a bit of a crush on Frank. He'd always been bewilderingly kind to her, even when she'd borrowed five thousand dollars for rent and never paid it back. He worked for the ACLU, fighting for prisoners' rights—perhaps her crimes had seemed small in comparison.

It had been so long—months and months and months—since a man had touched her. Sometimes Jess felt so lonely that her body ached.

She helped the kids into their costumes, zipping Floyd into his saber-tooth getup and tying Ellory's red-and-yellow striped tie. She was Hermione, of course. The girl stared at the wall, gravely, while Jess applied some mascara to her lashes. Ellory asked her if she'd read the books.

"I've seen the movies," Jess said, forcing herself to smile. "All eight of them. In fact, I watched them all in a row."

"At once?"

"Yes. A Harry Potter marathon."

Ellory seemed impressed. One of the few perks of major depression was that your lifestyle—excessive TV watching, a reluctance to bathe or brush your teeth—impressed children.

"What are you going to be?" Ellory asked.

"What?"

"Your *costume*."

Floyd dragged a bin from his room and pulled out a rubber mask. It seemed important to the kids that Jess dress up; she would do this for them, despite the treacherous mood that had descended upon her at the hospital. She tugged the mask over her head, peering at herself in the black mirror of the TV screen: an alien, with giant tree-frog eyes and a cleft head that looked mysteriously like someone's ass. It was hideous, this ass. And yet part of her preferred herself this way, as an ass-martian. No one would mistake her for someone they might want to invite over for brunch.

Outside, the streets were filled with kids, all of them, it seemed, dressed as characters from Harry Potter. Jess saw two other Hermiones, but the preponderance of plucky girl wizards did not seem to bother Ellory a bit. She and Floyd ran ahead, plastic pumpkins bumping their thighs. The sidewalk was covered in purple flowers that stuck to Jess's shoes. It was so warm out, the smell of jacaranda so pee-like and pervasive, that Jess began to sweat inside her mask. Some of the houses looked like they'd been decorated by Hollywood set designers, which, of course, they had: there was a giant UFO with eerie green light coming from its ramp, a pirate ship with cannons belching smoke, a cemetery with movie ghosts slithering out of the graves. Jess followed Floyd and Ellory from door to door, happy she didn't have to do any smiling from inside her alien head. All business, Floyd and Ellory didn't smile either. They held out their pumpkins to receive their due, good little pawns of the confectionary-industrial complex. No wonder Americans grew up so entitled, demanding things from strangers; before long you were invading countries and feeling insulted if they didn't fork over some treats.

They stopped at another yard done up like a cemetery. An animatronic skeleton popped out of a coffin, and the blob of trick-or-treaters that had surrounded it shrieked with pleasure. Jess hoped the children's joy would lift her spirits, but it seemed to have the opposite effect. The sidewalk pitched gently under her feet. She felt thirsty and uncaged. A pint-size Spider-Man turned to her and said, "Trick or treat," lifting his pumpkin like a beggar's bowl. What did the little twerp think? She was a walking vending machine?

"Trick," Jess said.

"What?"

"You gave me a choice. Let's see what kinds of tricks you can do."

Spider-Boy stared at her. "I don't know any tricks."

"Then you'd better think about what you're saying. You're walking around regurgitating something you don't even understand."

The kid backed away from her, then ran off to join his friends up the block. Jess glanced at Ellory, who was mouthing something to Floyd.

"What did you say?" Jess demanded.

Ellory stared into her pumpkin.

"You said something with your lips."

"She called you 'Aunt Mess,'" Floyd explained.

Ellory looked stricken.

"My dad calls you that sometimes," Floyd said.

"He does?"

"He said we should be getting paid to babysit you instead. He gave me a dollar. It's a joke," Floyd said judiciously, "but I get to keep it."

Jess felt weak. "And your mom finds this hilarious too?"

Ellory shushed Floyd before he could say more. Jess tugged at her mask, which had begun to feel like a guillotine hood. She had an image of Margot's family sitting around the dinner table, betting on what priceless thing Aunt Mess would do next. Go back to bed for six months? Splatter her brains all over the closet? The skeleton in its coffin continued to resurrect and die, resurrect and die, as if it found life and death equally unappealing. She turned away from the skeleton and bumped into a kid with a knife through his head. His mouth was covered in blood, as if he'd been feasting on an antelope. When he saw Jess staring at him, the boy grabbed one end of the knife—the handle—and began staggering around, pulling himself by the head.

Jess's legs felt strange. In fact, she was shrinking. The trees, the lampposts, the cars parked along the street—they seemed to inflate around her, swelling with breath. A rubber spider, as large as an Alaskan king crab, clung to the fence across the street. Jess leaned against a tree. A zombie with rotting cheeks ran past her, yelling, "I got a chocolate eyeball!" Nearby, a princess took out her teeth and began to eat them. Jess tried to reason her way back to health—she was well, weller than before, she was on a drug called Wellbutrin—but it was too late. She was curling at the edges, hardening into a Dink.

She sat down on the curb. She'd promised Dr. Zwelling not to give in to temptation, but now she pictured her emergency exit: the blade sliding across her throat, blood splattering the street. Her niece and nephew sat down beside her—or so it sounded like. One of them dumped candy onto the sidewalk and began to pan noisily for something. Jess did not know how long they sat there. It must have been some time, because when she opened her eyes Ellory was staring at her.

"Are you okay, Aunt Jess?" she asked.

Jess shook her head.

"You slid your finger, like, across your throat."

"I did?"

Ellory nodded. She looked frightened. Jess glanced beyond her at the puddle of candy on the sidewalk.

"Where's Floyd?"

Ellory looked around. "He was here. Eating a candy bar."

Jess grabbed her arm, somehow yanking them both to their feet. The streets were filled with children. "What kind was it?" Jess hissed.

"I don't know."

"Was it a Snickers?"

Ellory stared at the sidewalk.

"Jesus Christ," Jess said. "Aren't you supposed to be smart?"

Ellory winced. Jess was hurting her. She let go of her niece's arm and grabbed her by the wrist instead, scanning both sides of the street for signs of Floyd. Witches, Harry Potters, a snot-faced bumblebee—but no saber-tooths. Perhaps he'd gone on to the next house. Jess raced down the sidewalk, dragging Ellory along behind her—people were looking at them: an Angry Bird, the rapist from *A Clockwork Orange*—but the next house was dark. Jess charged down the block. He was not at the next house, or the next. In her mind's eye, Floyd's face began to swell into a pumpkin, his throat closing in anaphylactic shock. Perhaps he was already dead. She searched behind an acacia tree, pulling Ellory as if her niece were something on wheels, a wagon or a suitcase, her hand slick with sweat, threatening to slide off the girl's wrist, and so Jess gripped her even harder and stopped at the corner of a deserted playground and shouted Floyd's name, greeted by a vast and bugless quiet. A siren Dopplered by in the distance. The size of the world revealed itself, perhaps for the first time.

Jess closed her eyes, trying to catch her breath. Aunt Mess. The name did not do her justice. Only a complete fucking shambles could kill a four-year-old boy.

Something tugged at her: Ellory. The girl was pointing at the last house they'd passed. A man in a Viking helmet waved at them from the steps. Floyd was there too—or else his saber-toothed double—holding a Twizzler and play-fighting with a second boy dressed as a pirate.

"Dalton's house," Ellory said.

"Dalton?"

"His best friend. He must have gone inside or something."

Jess tried to pull Ellory toward her, ragged with relief, but the girl wriggled out of her grasp and drew back, clutching her wrist. Her own niece was afraid of her. Not upset or pissed off—but afraid. Ellory ran up the steps of the house, a beautiful Craftsman with a rubber skeleton hanging in one window. Jess was too sick inside, too speechless with remorse, to follow. Ellory kissed her brother on the head and began rummaging through a metal bowl of candy on the porch. Jess bent down to adjust one of her sandals; when she looked up, the man in the Viking helmet was coming toward her, trotting down the steps in flip-flops. He moved briskly, as if he had something to tell her. Had they met at one of Margot's parties? Years ago, perhaps? It seemed possible. He stopped in front of her, helmet tipped back like a yarmulke. His face was bearded and handsome. Poking out from below his beard was the bayonet of an Adam's apple, the pointiest one she'd ever seen.

She could smell the beer on his breath. He was standing that close. Jess started to say something, but the man's face, so impudently serious, mesmerized her. He reached out and touched her crotch, gripping it like a bowling ball. She was too startled to move.

"You're torturing me," the man whispered. "I can't sleep."

Jess's heart was skipping. A wildness in her chest.

"I can still taste your cunt."

She stepped back.

"Is Frank's mother still here? Can you sneak out tonight?"

Jess nodded, afraid to speak. She felt dizzy. The man turned around and jogged back to the house, where Ellory was still picking through the bowl of candy. Floyd and the boy he was playing with stabbed the man with their Twizzlers, and he stumbled backward, performing as if for an audience. For Jess. It was only when she remembered the mask, feeling the dampness of her breath inside it, that she realized there'd been a mistake.

Back at Margot's place, Jess turned on every light in the house, including the bathroom's. She was still trembling. It crossed her mind, even, to call the police. Of course, the mistake made sense: she was out with her sister's kids, dressed like an alien. Why would it have occurred to him she wasn't Margot? Still, it felt like an assault. Not just on her, Jess, but on her sister. If Margot and her neighbor were having an affair—which, unless the man was a lunatic, they clearly were—it was an assault on her marriage as well.

How was it possible, then, that even *this*—Margot's tawdry affair with a sex-crazed dad—made her jealous?

Jess went into Ellory's room to change. She needed to do this, to get out of the jeans she was wearing. Her niece had been sitting on the toilet for the past thirty minutes—"the porcelain babysitter," Margot called it, one of her few jokes—and had yet to emerge. Jess had asked her several times if she was all right and had been met with silence. She opened Ellory's art chest, which her niece had cleared out so she'd have a place for her clothes. That the girl had done this, anticipating her arrival, now seemed like a farce.

"Quite a haul," Margot said when she got home, bending down to kiss Floyd's head. Candy, like debris from a storm, covered the floor of the living room. Floyd slapped a hand over his eyes and nose and mouth and began to squeeze them together, groaning strangely, as if trying to tear off his face. He'd eaten too much sugar. No doubt Margot would add this to her inventory of Jess's failures. *A four-year-old boy, her own nephew, and Aunt Mess let him stuff his face with candy!* Frank would shake his head in disbelief.

Frank, Margot's cuckolded husband.

How strange it felt, to have this weapon at her disposal.

"Great," Margot said, when Jess asked how Frank was doing. "They're extremely optimistic. About the no lasting damage, I mean." She smiled, but there was something wrong with it. Perhaps Jess had seen too many costumes that evening, but the smile seemed to have been painted onto her face. "How was trick-or-treating?"

"We went to that big Craftsman on the corner," Jess said, picking a box of Milk Duds off the floor. "Dalton's house? I think the man there thought I was you."

Margot looked at her for the first time. She was no longer smiling. In fact, she was standing perfectly still. Amazingly, Jess had opened the box of Milk Duds and was about to pop one in her mouth. She put it back and closed the box.

"What did he say?" Margot asked.

"He was, um, very friendly."

Jess immediately wanted to take it back. That was the thing about revenge: it always made you feel worse. Margot stared at her, and for a moment something moved between them, as slow and silent as a breath. Jess looked into the damp lamps of Margot's eyes and saw for the first time in however many years the brain that was lighting them, the accumulation of fears and longings and regrets that somehow formed a substance, the mysterious thing that distinguished us from zombies and saber-tooths. Jess took a step toward her. There were some gray hairs in her sister's bangs—Jess had never noticed them before.

Margot looked away finally, breaking the spell. "It's not as easy as it looks."

It was not a confession, and yet the house felt quieter, as when a fan you hadn't noticed was running switches off. Floyd began to sing a song from *Grease*, something his sister had taught him, and Margot steadied herself against the couch. Jess touched her hand. How small it was! She might have been sixteen again: Jess's beautiful older sister. Jess remembered the time Margot had broken up with her boyfriend, Bobby Climan, how he'd convinced the eleventh graders at Sherman High that she was a slut. For a week or two, the vents of her locker were stuffed with lewd drawings and STD pamphlets. What sublime, grateful power Jess had felt, rocking her older sister in her arms while she wept into her shoulder.

Margot stared at their hands, as if they might scamper off the top of the couch. "Sometimes I wish it was me who had the brain tumor—lying there in bed, all that time to myself, someone to make sure I get *my* vitamins for a change."

"It's not all it's cracked up to be," Jess said. "Lying in bed all day."

Margot blushed. "Yeah. Right. I'm sorry." She was trembling now herself. She pulled her hand away and turned to Floyd, clearly eager to change the subject. "Speaking of bed, time to get you out of that tiger costume."

" 'Cat,' you mean," Jess said.

"*Cat.* I'm sorry."

"Ellory would have your head."

Margot surprised her by laughing. "I know. Honestly, she drives me crazy sometimes."

Jess floated with relief. "Today she corrected my grammar. My grammar! I said 'between you and I,' and she corrected me."

"Frank encourages her," Margot said. "He thinks she's on her way to Harvard."

"We'll see about that. When she asked about the N-word, in the car, I told her it means 'best friend.' "

Margot laughed. It was the two of them again, huddled in the backseat.

"And what about the way she preens in the mirror? Did we do that at her age? *My hair, my beautiful hair.*" Jess imitated Ellory, fluffing her hair and shaking her head like someone in a shampoo commercial. "Those teeth are adorable now, but in five years—I hate to say it— they're going to cost you a fortune."

Margot stiffened. She'd gone too far. Before Jess could repair the damage, Ellory emerged from the bathroom with her face buried in *Harry Potter and the Goblet of Fire.* She sat down on the couch and began to take off her Hermione robe, balancing the open book in her lap. A bruise braceleted her wrist. Jess prayed that Margot wouldn't notice, but she reached down and touched it. Ellory flinched.

Jess had no choice but to explain about Floyd's disappearance, how she'd dragged Ellory around in a panic. "I was worried he'd eaten a Snickers," she said, knowing how it must sound.

"She called me stupid too," her niece said, refusing to look at her.

"I did not!"

"She tried to break my wrist."

"I never tried to do that!"

Margot glanced from Jess to Ellory and then back to Jess again, as if trying to make up her mind who to believe. Of course, she knew what Ellory was like—she'd admitted it herself. No way a seven-year-old's word would stand up in court. Jess sensed this in Margot's face: a hesitation, or in any case a reluctance to return to her role of perfect mom.

"She's not my mother," Ellory said, as if she might cry. "I want her to go home."

Jess did something she couldn't explain. She made a face at her niece. Curled her lip up and stuck her front teeth out, twitching her nose like a rabbit. It was hideous, loathsome, exhilarating.

Margot, staring at her, enfolded Ellory in her arms. Her eyes darkened.

"What the hell is wrong with you?" She didn't sound amazed this time—only sad. She shook her head. "I can't do it," Margot said, tightening her grip on her daughter. "I'm sorry you're in despair. I am. But I can't take care of anyone else."

Jess couldn't sleep, terrorized by visions of slitting her own throat. An endless movie clip. "Ideation," Dr. Zwelling called it, as if it were something she could control, but in fact her brain was a multiplex and she was no longer the projectionist. Jess thought of the movie that had played the afternoon she tried to kill herself. After gobbling all the Vicodin—ten minutes later? an hour?—she'd looked up and seen a naked woman standing at the foot of her bed. The woman was old and wrinkled, and it took Jess a second to recognize herself. Her breasts were like flaps, like sleeping eyes. The woman, the old Jess, smiled at her. Jess was not appalled or horrified but filled with a strange feeling of peace. *You'll be happy someday,* the feeling seemed to promise, and she had called 911 to find out for herself.

But it was a movie, of course—nothing more. The old hag had tricked her.

Jess got up eventually and slipped into her clothes. *In despair,* Margot had said. Such a romantic term, "despair"—Jess had always hated its air of existential chic. (Where were the Bertolucci movies about "depression": Brando watching *The Andy Griffith Show* in the middle of the day?) And yet depression *was* romantic, in its own gruesome way. A lifelong devotion. Margot had married her postcollege sweetheart; Jess had married hers too. They were in it together, till death do them part.

Jess stopped at her sister's door, long enough to hear the flamboyant rattle of her snores. She had always snored this way, like a rhinoceros. Jess did not think she could feel any sadder, but the sound of her sister's snores proved her wrong. It was like hanging your heart on a hook and watching it die.

Sometimes, as a kid, she'd tried to will herself into Margot's body, tried to climb her sister's snores like a ladder and become the beautiful girl sleeping in the bunk above her. As she'd lain there in the dark, deranged by exhaustion, it had seemed almost possible.

Now, in the hallway, Jess closed her eyes and indulged in the old, soothing fantasy. Here were her beloved children. Here was her bland, expensive house. Here were the money and the friendships and the reasons to crawl out of bed, no better or worse than any others. Here—just down the street—was her handsome, kinky lover, dreaming about the taste of her cunt.

Jess grabbed the alien mask from the coat hook in the front hall and tugged it over her head, breathing in its dizzying toxins. A dark excitement fluttered in her chest. She slipped out the front door and headed to the sidewalk. She felt wide awake, as if someone had doused her with water. She passed the neighbors' yards, which were still and quiet now, the decorations already beginning to seem out of place. The skeleton had ceased its merry resurrections and lay inside its coffin, sleeping peacefully, like the dutiful wives tucked inside their homes. Little did these wives know. Or perhaps they did know. Yes—gossip was afoot, she'd enlarged their lives through her own deceit. She walked down the street and stopped at the Craftsman on the corner.

The porch light was off, a few stray Kisses glittering on the moonlit steps. She knocked on the door. A light flipped on in the house, then another one outside. Her lover laughed when he saw the mask.

"I'd given up hope," he said.

How beautiful he was, as tall and fine-boned as a movie star. As soon as she thought this, she wondered if it might be true: He was an actor in the movies. A Hollywood widower. His wife had killed herself. She followed him into the living room, which was a mess. Coke cans littered the coffee table, and on the rug in front of the TV was a pizza box containing fingers of crust. His hair was thinning in back,

67

cycloning around a bald spot. Even the bald spot seemed beautiful, like an infant's. They stopped in front of the TV, which was playing softly. An orange cat trickled down the stairs and began to rub against her legs. She stared up at the darkness beyond the staircase.

"Asleep," the man said.

She was breathless, but not from fear. The man's Adam's apple bobbed into his beard. *Margot,* he said. A rare feeling—joy, perhaps—flooded her veins. The man tried to grab her mask, but she didn't let him take it off. He squinted at her in surprise, then grinned. She found the light switch on the wall and turned it off. She could not go down on him with the mask on, but that was all right; she'd do other things, whatever he wanted. He stopped grinning. His face, in the blue light of the TV, glowed like a flower. She was expecting it to take longer, given his earlier promises, but before long he lifted her dress from behind and bent her over the couch. This was something she was used to, a fuck in the dark. And then it wasn't. Something had changed, a shift in his attack: it was slower somehow, more tentative, less worshipful than astonished. She wasn't Margot anymore. But of course she wasn't Jess either. She hadn't been Jess for a long time. She remembered playing hide-and-seek with Margot when they were kids, how once she'd hidden herself so well under the storm hatch to the basement that Margot couldn't find her, not for five minutes and then ten and then so long she started to go a little bit crazy, time stretching out like taffy, her sister's steps creaking right above her head, and she began to wonder if anyone would ever find her, if she hadn't somehow disappeared for good. The man let go of her, as if to stop, but she thrust backward into him and he grabbed her in a different way, more roughly this time, as if they'd agreed upon something, and she drifted from her body and rose up to the ceiling and could see the scene perfectly: a woman with an alien's head, making noises, the human behind her making noises too. Jess drifted even higher, dangling perilously in the sky, imagining she could see into the bedrooms of the neighbors' houses as well, into bedrooms all over the city, every one of them occupied by couples with the same problem: they had no idea who they were fucking.

Afterward, the man had trouble buttoning his pants. He seemed rattled, ashamed to look at her, but there was something else in his face too. An emotion she couldn't place.

"Who are you?"

Jess shook her head. She stepped toward him, but he flinched away and switched on the lights. His mouth tucked into a frown. That's what she'd seen on his face: disappointment. Maybe even disgust.

"Whoever you are," he said. "Whoever the fuck you are. Get out of my house."

Jess backed away from him. Turning, she raced out the door and half tripped down the front steps and then headed into the road. Her face itched inside the mask. An electrical box buzzed from a pole. The air seemed to hum with transmissions. Jess followed the road and didn't look back. Why she was walking in the street, she couldn't say. It seemed like the best way to get home. She didn't know where it was, this home, but they cooked rocks there and ate them for dinner. *I'm lost,* people said, but what if there was nothing inside of you—nothing good or true or valuable—to lose?

Some distant lights swung in her direction, growing brighter as she walked toward them. She lay down in the middle of the road. Remarkably, the asphalt was still warm. The warmth felt good to her.

The lights grew brighter, illuminating the eucalyptus tree in someone's yard. There was a dwelling inside the tree, an amazing contrivance of planks and ladders. It looked like something a lunatic, or a happy person, might build. Jess closed her eyes, waiting for the lights to arrive, but they turned up a driveway and left her lying there in the dark. A door slammed, then another; voices drifted into a house. She lay there for a long time, but no more lights appeared. She was trapped on earth.

At Margot's house, the lights were still off, as if nothing had happened. Jess took off her mask and dropped it in the trash can in the kitchen. How long she stood there, she couldn't be sure. She felt like she might throw up. On the wall above the trash can was a poster that Ellory had made at school. Jess could just make it out in the dark. THINGS THAT ARE WRONG WITH THE WORLD, it was called.

Margot's bedroom door was wide open now. Jess peered inside and saw Floyd sleeping on top of his mother's chest: a boy in dinosaur pajamas, riding the gentle swells of Margot's snores. She looked as beautiful as always, hair pooled around her head like a mermaid's. Floyd jerked suddenly and caught his breath, but Margot didn't stir. Her face seemed younger in the dark, almost childlike. Her eyelids flickered, or seemed to, and Jess wondered whether she was dreaming about the man down the street.

For the first time in years, Jess did not feel envious of her. This was an odd feeling, like waking up in a room you'd forgotten was there. All the boys Margot had dated as a teenager, the delirium that Jess had taken for happiness: what if it hadn't been that at all?

Jess closed her sister's door softly and then went to the bathroom.

It hurt when she peed. She hadn't felt sore like this in a long time. She thought about taking a bath—it was what she used to do in the old days, to soak off the grubbiness of a strange fuck—but this time she wanted to feel grubby inside.

She got her bag out of the closet. There was a Comfort Inn on Sunset. She would leave right away—no reason to wait till morning. She did not want to talk to Margot or have to go through the motions of reconciliation.

She tiptoed into her niece's room to get her clothes out of the chest. Like her mother, Ellory was lost in sleep, her face softened by the glow of the night-light. The room smelled touchingly of farts. Beside her in bed, arranged from thinnest to fattest, was a miniature staircase of Harry Potter books. Jess used to hide Laura Ingalls Wilder novels under her covers so she could read them after Margot and their parents fell asleep. Quietly, she opened the chest at the foot of Ellory's bed and began to pack her clothes into the roller bag.

"What are you doing?" Ellory asked. She was watching from bed, blinking at Jess with puffy eyes.

"Sorry. Go back to sleep."

"Are you going back to the hotel?" Ellory said.

She seemed to have inherited Margot's ability to vault out of sleep, like a cat. Jess wished she were still lying in the street. Her heart, for some reason, was pounding.

"It wasn't a hotel."

"What was it?"

"A place for people like me," she said. "People who try to hurt themselves."

Ellory sat up in bed. "Did you try to hurt yourself?"

Jess nodded.

"Why?"

She turned back to her bag, laying a stack of underwear inside. What could she say? That she'd tried to walk to Starbucks one day and had seen a row of medical scooters lined up on the sidewalk, the kind that sick and obese people ride around on? The medical scooters, sitting in front of one of those wretched places that sell crutches and walkers, had helium balloons tied to them. Partly, Jess couldn't stand the idea of seeing those scooters again.

"It's hard to explain."

Ellory chewed her lip, then glanced at Jess and covered her front teeth. God, what had she done? On the bedside table was the plastic wand from Ellory's costume.

"There's something wrong with your brain," Ellory said quietly, as if it had just occurred to her.

"Yes."

Jess was astonished to see a tear, black with mascara, leaking from her niece's eye.

"Is my dad going to be all right?"

"Of course," Jess said, though in truth she had no idea. She had accepted Margot's version of things without giving it a second thought. She walked around the foot of the bed and sat next to her niece. "Yes, absolutely."

"I keep having bad thoughts. Like he's going to die." Ellory swiped her eyes with the back of her hand. "There's something wrong with my brain too."

Mascara bruised her cheeks. It seemed unspeakable to Jess, that this was her niece's first experience with running makeup. What would Margot do? Kiss the top of Ellory's head. Talk to her in a special voice, the lilting baritone of love: *Sweetie, Ell-Ell, there's nothing wrong.* Jess was about to do this but then had a different idea, a better one. She grabbed the wand from the bedside table and pointed it at Ellory's head.

"Extracto," she said, pretending to siphon her thoughts.

"No, that's not it," her niece said. She pulled the wand closer to her head. "Dumbledore just does it. There's no magic word."

Jess let herself be bossed. This was what being a mother was, pretending to cast a spell when you were really under someone else's. She touched the wand to Ellory's head and imagined the CGI effects, a fonduey string of light sucked from her niece's brain. How impressed Margot would be, if she were watching from the doorway. Jess summoned this fantasy and then did her best to reject it. She could not remember the last time she'd helped someone simply because they needed it.

She stood up and tugged her dress down, smoothing the wrinkles over her stomach, and a strange thought occurred to her. What if she got pregnant? A half-alien thing, neither human nor martian, so awful it made people gasp. It did not frighten Jess, this fantasy. A Halloween baby. It would be shunned and monstrous, something that could love her.

Jess looked out the window at the terraced orchard of the backyard. Fruit lay rotting on the ground. An empty lawn chair sat in the middle of the grass, floating on a pond of moonlight. She would remember this moment, as clear and incorruptible as a song. The empty chair. The pure, beckoning silence. The moonlit grass and the faint singe of stars and the trees that, though winter was coming, hadn't lost a single leaf.

"Everything's going to be fine," Jess said.

"Promise?"

Her niece was watching her, wide awake now—a girl with her whole life in front of her. Jess placed the toy wand back on the table. She could tell the truth, or she could be a grown-up for once.

"Promise," Jess said.

INDEPENDENCE

It all started when Rogelio staple-gunned a flyer to a guy's chest at Being and Books. Or maybe that was the end of things, I don't know. It's been a strange year, full of love and despair.

Here's what happened: Customer wanted a book. Customer approached Employee and asked for a recommendation for his teen-age son, who "likes Star Wars books and stuff like that."

Employee: Science fiction?

Customer: Yeah. Maybe.

Employee: Is he more of a sword-and-planet guy, or is he into cyberpunk?

Customer: Swords, I think.

Employee: So science fantasy?

Customer: Uh-huh. Maybe. Also, catalogs—he likes looking through those.

Unbidden, Customer explained that he was divorced and feeling estranged from his son, with whom he hoped to connect "on a deeper level." Instead of stating the obvious (e.g., "your son's a moron and you're better off keeping the level where it is"), Employee spent fifteen minutes looking for the perfect book that would save Customer from heartbreak while also kindling in his son a lifelong love of reading. And did Employee find it? Of course. A science fantasy about—you guessed it—a father-and-son dragon-riding team. *Only together, reunited at the edge of time, do they stand a chance of defeating the Emperor of Flurg.* In hardcover, no less, so Customer's son wouldn't take him for a cheapskate.

And what did Customer do? How did he thank Employee for his time? Whipped out his smartphone and looked the book up on Amazon and then . . . *he ordered it in the fucking store.*

How do I know this? Because I'm the employee. I spied on him from behind the Staff Picks.

That's when Employee—I—went over and told Rogelio what had happened. He was working with Lalima, hanging up a flyer for an Isaac Babel lecture, meaning Lalima was holding the flyer against the wall and he was leaning into her back to staple-gun the corners. Lalima was basically the reason Rogelio and I'd found to keep living. Plenty of beautiful young women read David Foster Wallace, but how many walk around with *Middlemarch* in their purses? How many love cheap beer and listen to Merle Haggard records and have freckled noses even though they're of Indian descent? The three of us were best friends until one lonely afternoon a week before Rogelio's meltdown, when she kissed me in the Being and Books bathroom. It was a small kiss—more speculative fiction than dirty realism—but Rogelio sensed something in the air and immediately began to make his move.

Now he pulled away from Lalima and looked at me, his bony

shoulders winged back as if he were preparing to clock me in the face. He'd worked at Being and Books since college and didn't take kindly to "collaborators," as he called them, though usually his hatred was seasoned with a dash of pity. There was no pity in Rogelio's face now. His nostrils actually trembled. On the sound system the Modern Lovers were singing "Roadrunner," one of Lalima's favorites. *I'm in love with modern moonlight.*

Then he turned and marched through Cultural Criticism and found the guy smiling at his phone, shaking his head at something on the screen. Rogelio lifted the staple gun. It was a serious instrument, one of those heavy-duty numbers, and he brandished it like a pistol. In the other fist was a flyer he'd grabbed from his stack. The song ended and a strange silence, deep as space, filled the store. When the man failed to look up, Rogelio slapped the flyer to the guy's chest and then stuck the gun to him like a defibrillator and in one swift, bold, surprisingly elegant motion pulled the trigger over his heart.

You know those old cartoons where someone's mouth opens so wide it eats the back of his head? The guy screamed without scream-ing. Then his voice switched on again and he did his best to make up for it, running around the store and yelling bloody murder, a red stain seeping across Isaac Babel's face. To be honest, it was a pretty good advertisement for his prose style. Rogelio and I watched in a kind of trance. Thank god for Lalima, who had the presence of mind to call 911.

Needless to say, the incident didn't help Being and Books with its struggle for solvency. The guy pressed charges against Rogelio and threatened to sue, but that's not the worst of it. Hersch, the owner, had no choice but to let Rogelio go. It broke Hersch's heart to do this, I could tell. We were like a family: a triracial, incestuous, downwardly mobile family, but a family nonetheless. Lalima and I waited in New Releases while Hersch talked to Rogelio in the back. When they emerged, Hersch wouldn't meet my eye, his normally pink face looking gray and old. His ponytail had come loose from its band. I didn't know who I felt worse for. It was Hersch who'd taken us in after college, who'd given us work and encouragement and a sense of belonging—who'd seen in Rogelio, especially, a possible heir.

There'd been a rift between them lately, it was true, about how to save the store. For Hersch, it was the artisanal angle. He saw hope in the gourmet donut shops, the pop-up clothing stores, the handcrafted axes being sold on the Internet.

"What do you want to do?" Rogelio said. "Change Used Books to Heritage Books?"

"I'm just trying to compete," Hersch said. "People want beautiful things."

"Walt Whitman? William Butler Yeats? That's not beautiful enough for them?"

Hersch looked at him. "When's the last time we sold a book of poetry?"

Hersch's idea for the store was to hire local artists to make handmade sleeves for literary classics: no two would be the same, and of course Amazon wouldn't be able to undersell them. "So you want to turn Dostoyevsky into coffee-table art?" Rogelio said incredulously. He was still upset when we went to lunch, muttering to himself on the sidewalk. Lalima did her best to talk him down, draping her arm over his shoulder as we walked to the taqueria. Maybe I thought this was a bit much. Maybe I thought she was overcompensating. It was a warm afternoon, not a hint of June gloom, and she was wearing a dress that showed the faint down on her spine. Our bathroom kiss had been the day before, and I guess I felt like any arm draping should involve me.

I should clarify something: Rogelio, for all his brilliance, had never had a girlfriend. For one thing, he's very skinny. His nickname in college was Stick Man. Girls pretty much ignored him, but he didn't seem to mind all that much. Books were his true lovers. He dumped a fair number of them, in anger or betrayal, but had long, steamy affairs with the ones he loved: *Lipstick Traces*, *Pale Fire*, *Pedro Páramo*. When I met him on the third day of freshman orientation, during a game of Capture the Flag, he was carrying *Against Interpretation* around with him, wearing a secondhand suit jacket too big in the shoulders. He looked like he was going to a scarecrow wedding. Like me, he despised Capture the Flag. He didn't see the point in running after something just because other people were. We hit it off so well, I think—became best friends—because we were happy to sit around reading while other people did the capturing.

I was an ignoramus compared to Rogelio, and sometimes I think it was my lack of knowledge, or maybe taste, that bound us so deeply. He taught me which writers to love (Woolf, Borges) and which writers to hate (Wolfe, Kerouac), as if he were a soccer captain choosing teams. There was never any middle ground. Sometimes I'd read something he'd recommended—a Rilke poem, say—and it would mystify me, or at least its greatness would elude me, but then Rogelio would sit down with me and excavate its meanings, explaining why it was precise and mysterious at the same time, reading from it in his public-radio voice, so rich and biblical it sounded unreal. We spent many nights like this, huddled against the wall while our dormmates went to keg parties and brought girls (or boys) back to their rooms. Even later, when I started dating girls myself, Rogelio acted like he didn't care, like he preferred spending his Saturday night with Alyosha or Kinbote or whoever he was seeing at the time.

So when Lalima came along, it threw us both. Rogelio had been against hiring her at first—too "midlife crisis," he complained to Hersch, though I think he was just worried she wouldn't give him the time of day—and yet here was a woman who seemed to like *both* of us, someone smart and funny and almost as well read as he. Someone, in other words, worth capturing. We had great fun together at the store. Lalima hated "lyrical" prose—it was her pet peeve—and liked to read from egregious offenders in an evil genius voice that made us laugh. On days off we walked the streets of Silver Lake, pretending we'd stepped out of Steinbeck and couldn't understand what had happened to California. We liked to call iPhones "walkie-talkies," asking people if we could radio our mothers. We kept a list of "Useful Words & Phrases," things we'd overheard on the street: "Let's bucketize our thoughts" was on there, as was "Fuck, I screwed up my foam art!" This last one we'd heard at a café, while someone was Instagramming his cappuccino. It had turned into a running joke: if one of us—Rogelio, say—was having a crappy morning, he'd frown and mutter "My foam art," and Lalima and I would nod and squeeze his shoulder.

I mention all this only to explain why Lalima's arm around Rogelio interested me so much. It was a complicated arm. I looked forward to seeing it return to her side at lunch. When we got to Taqueria Sanchez, though, it was no longer Taqueria Sanchez. It was a place called Comida para la Vida. There were dairy-free horchatas, soy chorizo tacos, something called a Kale César salad.

"Where's the cabeza?" I asked the cashier, a white guy with tattoos sleeving his arms.

"We don't have that anymore, sorry."

"Grass-fed cabeza?"

"No cabeza at all. It's under new ownership."

"Where's Mr. Sanchez?" Lalima asked.

The cashier looked at her, then glanced back at a man grilling a green quesadilla and wearing an apron that said TACOS ARE GOOD FOR YOU. The world continually finds new ways to make you sad.

"Say a prayer for cabeza," I sighed, bumping Lalima with my ass. I'd never done anything like this before; if you'd asked me a second before it happened, I would have denied being an ass bumper of any kind. I glanced up and Rogelio was staring at me, looking like he'd stepped in something.

"What's this with you and cabeza?" he said. "You always talked about how disgusting it looked."

"That doesn't mean I wanted it to go away."

Rogelio curled his lip. We went to a Thai place on Sunset, but he refused to speak to us, staring into his drunken noodles while Lalima and I sat across from him in the booth, our legs nearly touching under the table. I caught his eye once, between slurps, and it looked like someone was tightening him with a winch. He was the best friend I'd ever had—the person, maybe, I most admired in the world—but suddenly I was fed up. Why did it always have to be this way with him? All or nothing? It wasn't my fault that Lalima had kissed me in the bathroom, just as it wasn't Hersch's fault he needed to appeal to hipsters. Rogelio wanted life to be precise and uncompromising, like a great novel. But life wasn't a great novel. It was vague and incongruous and poorly plotted. You compromised all the time.

I was hoping things would go back to normal at the store, especially because Lalima was helping Hersch run some numbers, but Rogelio went off by himself to process some returns. It was a slow day—most days were slow ones, to be honest—so I decided to surprise him with a round of Highly Specific Yet Obscure. This was a game we used to play. One of us would pretend to be a customer and come up with an outrageous request, the harder the better. It was good practice for the Christmas season. Rogelio, the reigning champ, had never once been stumped.

Now I thought I'd give him a chance to best me at something. A peace offering. If our friendship collapsed, it wouldn't be on me.

"Do you work here?" I asked him.

"I don't feel like playing," Rogelio said, bent over an invoice.

"I'm looking for a gift."

"Leave me alone."

I sighed. "I've been to twelve different bookstores. You probably couldn't help me anyway."

He looked up at me then—he never could resist the challenge—and narrowed his eyes. And as soon as he did, as soon as his eyes narrowed in their cocky, all-knowing, invincible way, something snagged in my chest. I wanted more than anything to beat him. I tried to think up something preposterous: a request from hell.

"All right," he said. "What is it?"

I cleared my throat. "A dog ate my face off and now I have the face of a dead person, you know, a donor's. She donated her face before she died."

"And?"

"Well, I need to buy a book for the dead person's daughter, to make her feel less creeped out that I have her mother's face."

I smirked at Rogelio, waiting for him to look flummoxed.

"I'm in a bit of a rush," I said.

"Come this way."

"I don't blame you for being stumped."

"Come this way!" he shouted.

First he led me into Psychology, where he grabbed R. D. Laing's *The Divided Self.* Clever, but not enough to shake my confidence. Still, Rogelio was just warming up. In Asian Lit he handed me a book called *Losing Face and Finding Grace,* which made me smile despite myself. I waited for him to smile back, to acknowledge the absurdity of my challenge, but he wasn't done, this was his reason for being, to make little cities out of books, each one a bridge to the next, and so he swung without breaking his stride and ushered me to Pet Care, where he tossed me *Feed Your Pet Right: The Authoritative Guide to Feeding Your Dog and Cat,* and then on to Cooking to pull out *The Omnivore's Dilemma.* I laughed—I couldn't help it. By now Lalima and Hersch had caught wind of something, and they emerged from the back office to watch. I explained my request on the way to Children's, where Rogelio handed me *Are You My Mother?,* which led him to *That's Not Your Mommy Anymore: A Zombie Tale,* a book I'd never even seen before, and then into his bread and butter, Used Fiction, where the books came fast and furious: *The Anatomy Lesson, The Double, Family Resem-*

blances. He was surfing the bookstore, making connections a computer couldn't, and it was beautiful to watch—we were his audience, his apostles, led further into a kingdom of his making. He pirouetted into Crime, where he grabbed *The Talented Mr. Ripley* before doubling back for *The Scarlet Pimpernel,* a pairing that baffled me for a second before I turned with my tower of books and explained that they were both about impersonation, and Hersch and Lalima grinned, we were all weirdly triumphant, for Rogelio's quest had become something else, a paean to Being and Books, to the promise that you could piece together a life story with books, with our books and our knowledge and our pure, glorious skill, and glowing with pride Rogelio veered into Lit Crit and topped my stack off with *The Power of Thetis: Allusion and Interpretation in the Iliad,* which stumped me until he said, "Thetis, the *immortal mother* of Achilles," and it was like he was describing the bookstore itself, our immortal mother, which would live on and take care of us forever, no matter what she looked like.

And then, of course, Rogelio was fired. It's my fault, my fault. Some part of me knew—when I approached him about the customer ordering from Amazon, saw Rogelio turn to me with the staple gun—that no good would come of it.

But what I'll never forget about that day is what happened before he walked out of the store. He'd spent the afternoon at the police station and smelled like Tums and B.O. Rogelio stopped at the staff pick table and straightened a stack of *Lucky Jims.* "Let's go," he said to me in that improbable voice, the one that could make an owner's manual sound like music. "We're off the menu." It took me a second to real-

84

ize he wanted me to quit my job, to follow him out the door the way I'd come in. I glanced at Lalima, who was staring at the carpet, and I didn't move.

It's been six months now and no lawsuit has materialized. Being and Books is still hanging on. Hersch made a halfhearted effort to talk to some artists, to get them interested in his book-sleeve idea, but so far nothing's come of it. Even so, customers wander in, sipping their lattes. The bell on the door jingles. We had a strong Christmas this year, enough to get us through the summer.

Still, it's not the same without Rogelio around. He was the *pneuma* of Being and Books, the breath that filled its lungs. Sometimes, Lalima will read something in her evil genius voice that makes me laugh and I'll glance around for Rogelio, forgetting for a second he isn't there, and my heart will slip a notch. He won't return my calls. When I go by his apartment, no one's ever home.

"Does Hersch seem okay to you?" Lalima says to me one day at lunch.

"What do you mean?"

"He seems old. His eyes are starting to look old-guy watery. The other day I asked if we had *Tropic of Cancer* in stock, and he asked me who it was by."

We're holding hands at the table, waiting for our food. We've started going to the taqueria down the street, the one that serves soy chorizo tacos. Though neither of us will admit it out loud, the food's better than it used to be. When our tacos arrive, Lalima puts the plate in her lap and leans back against me in the booth.

That's when I see him, Rogelio, through the open window. He's walking down the sidewalk with his face in a book. God knows what it is: Calvino, maybe, or Pynchon, or Highsmith. He's skinnier than I've ever seen him—which is very skinny—and his hair looks greasy and disheveled. People have actually stopped looking at their phones and are moving to get out of *his* way. He clears a path down the sidewalk—probably he has no idea where he is—and there's something beautiful about him, something rare and slow and possessed: a man lost inside a book. I open my mouth to call to him, but I don't. I don't. I just miss him when he disappears.

EXPRESSION

When I was fifteen I wrote a short story for Ms. Nowinski's English class called "The Infants' Masada." I'd found the word "Masada" while flipping through the encyclopedia, in search of a title, and it was love at first sight. Right away I knew it would lend the necessary gravitas to my story, which was told from the perspective of a newborn on a premature baby ward. Inexplicably, the preemie had a full vocabulary. He also had a precocious attraction to his favorite nurse, Ingrid, who sang to him every night in a "plaintive voice." Late one night, awake in his incubator, the preemie watches Ingrid get raped by one of the doctors at the hospital. He lies there helpless as she struggles, unable to intervene. Afterward, he decides he would rather freeze to death than face such a cruel and predatory world. The preemie makes a fist and, summoning all his strength, punches through the glass case of his incubator. Inspired by this brave act of protest, the other preemies on the ward punch through their incubators as well, a forest of tiny arms. This is the denouement.

Ms. Nowinski gave me an A plus and wrote in her comments that my story was "a poignant expression of human cruelty as well as a brilliant retelling of Jewish history." This last part stumped me—I wasn't Jewish and had nearly failed World History—but the rest I could relate to. I was all about poignant expressions of human cruelty, especially if they appealed to women. Until then, the nicest comment I'd gotten at school was from Mr. Gerbino, my Earth Science teacher, who'd said that I showed "a firm grasp of weather systems."

My father, too, was impressed by the story—so impressed, in fact, that he decided to send me to arts camp. This turned out to be a summer camp for "artistically inclined youth." It was not in California, where we lived, but in Massachusetts.

"I don't want to be an artist," I said. I associated artists with the sorts of kids my mother described as "interesting." Plus I had a girlfriend, my first, and I'd been making some slow but promising headway with her on the trampoline in her backyard. The summer stretched before me like a vista of erotic suffering.

"Writers feed off experience," my father said. He'd been a French literature major in college and sometimes said things like this. "It nourishes their imagination."

My sister laughed, her mouth full of cornflakes. She was jealous because she didn't have a talent of her own. "For Christ's sake. He's fifteen years old."

"Rimbaud wrote his first immortal poem at fifteen," my father said.

"I want to be immortal at home," I said.

My father sighed.

"Mom and Dad want to go to Europe," my sister explained. "They're sending me off to Mexico for a month to help orphans."

So I ended up in Massachusetts, at a camp for artists. As it turned out, the camp was not really a camp at all, but a boarding school in the middle of nowhere that doubled in the summers as a place to dump your kids. My roommate was a boy named Chet Turnblad. I'd never met a Chet before and was impressed to discover he fulfilled all my expectations for the name. He had red hair and bad skin and one of those haircuts that looked like he'd sprinkled weed killer on the top and let the rest grow down to his shoulders. He'd moved into the dorm the day before and had decorated the wall over his bed with a poster of Miles Davis in an ascot, sitting backward in a chair with one leg slung insolently over the top. I knew a bit about jazz—my father had a stash of old records—but I'd never met anyone my age who listened to it on purpose. Facing the door, where everyone would see it as they came in, was another poster: a heavy metal band scowling at the camera, their hair permed into Louis XIV curls.

I decided Chet was from Kansas or Mississippi or somewhere else where they might send you away for listening to devil music. As it turned out, he lived in town. I was surprised. Riding the van in from the airport, I hadn't seen much of anything: farms, a few motels, then the lonely spire of a church and some deserted-looking shops hawking school souvenirs.

"You live nearby?" I asked.

"On Lincoln Road," he said. His voice was startling, too deep for his skinny frame, as if it had been dubbed from another language. "Near the lake."

"Don't you have your own room?"

"Sure."

He blushed, turning to the neat stacks of cassette tapes he'd arranged alphabetically on the bookcase. It made no sense to me that he would want to live in a dorm instead of his own house, particularly when it smelled like mouse turds and there was no air-conditioning and the humidity was making me leave skeletal footprints when I walked. I felt like my eyeballs might slide out of their sockets. I couldn't help thinking of my friends back in California, hanging out at the beach, basking in the cool ocean breeze before they hurled themselves deliciously into the water. This led me to my girlfriend: how her mouth tasted like the Diet Cokes she always drank, cold enough to numb my lips, each snowy kiss leaving a metallic sweetness on my tongue. Her name was Sylvana. It sounded like a country to me, some beautiful place I was perpetually on the verge of discovering. So far I'd only managed to glimpse the shore. Alone on the trampoline, her parents gone for the evening, we would kiss and grope and grind, dry-humping until I felt like crying.

After I'd unpacked my duffel bag in the miserable heat, Chet and I went to dinner. He was wearing a Red Sox cap that looked as if it had come right out of the box, stiff as plastic, his red hair fluffing out the back like the tail of a squirrel. I didn't really want to be seen with him, but I also didn't want to insult him on our first day, seeing as how we'd be living together all summer. The dinner was an orientation thing: everyone was given a painting, a little postcard, and you were supposed to sit at the table that had your painting on it. My postcard was of an old man staring adoringly into a kid's eyes. The man's nose was covered in revolting warty bumps, like one of those gourds people put out for Halloween. I was dispirited to see that Chet had the same painting. We got some Sloppy Joes from the buffet line and found our table in the far corner of the dining hall, a blowup of the man with the deformed nose clipped to an easel beside it. I glanced at the table next to us, who were dining in the company of a naked woman braiding her hair.

"What's wrong with his nose?" I said, laying my fork down. The Sloppy Joes—or maybe the hall itself—smelled like an old retainer. "It's grossing me out."

"It's a famous painting," said the boy sitting across from me. He had long black bangs grazing his eyelids and a smile that pushed his lips into a dolphiny beak. His name tag said ETHAN. "By Ghirlandaio."

"You think he would have left out the warts."

"Actually it's a skin condition," Ethan said. "They're little tumors."

"When I was nine I had this big tumor grow out of my back," said the girl next to me, whose glasses made her eyes float in front of her face. She'd stacked four bun bottoms on top of each other, layering them with several strata of orange glop, so that her Sloppy Joe resembled a wedding cake. "They did surgery and took it out and found human hair and teeth in it. It's called a teratoma. Sometimes they even have toes or fingers!"

"Wow," I said.

I glanced at Chet, who widened his eyes at me. I widened mine back. Already, I'd stopped caring so much what people thought of him. I glanced around the sweltering dining hall and saw an assortment of artistically inclined youth hunched over their Sloppy Joes, some of them dressed in black, a jumble of sweaty, homesick faces that looked no more interesting than I did. I suspected we were all here because our parents had preyed on our vanity in order to get us out of their hair. Beyond the condiment station, standing near the door, were two policemen sweating miserably in their uniforms.

"What's up with the cops?" I asked.

"The long arm of the law?" Ethan said. "Didn't you get the notice?"

I shook my head.

"The Dorm Room Prowler. Someone's been stealing things out of students' rooms. Early arrivals—foreigners, mostly. Preying on the weak and the German."

"We're supposed to lock our doors even when we go to the bathroom," the girl with the glasses explained.

"Who is it?"

Ethan shrugged, flipping the bangs from his eyes. "Some townie, I guess."

I looked at Chet, who was staring at his plate, eating peas by impaling one on each tine of his fork. Of the four of us, he was the only one who'd asked for a vegetable. On the way back to our room, Chet and I sweated across the quad while crickets trilled all around us, like a ten-speed singing downhill. The sun was going down and the air had begun to pulse with tiny specks of light. I'd never seen fireflies before, and it took me a minute to realize what they were. I had to admit it was a beautiful campus. The buildings were much older than anything we had at home, red-brick and stately and taller than the pulsing lights, and the clock tower looming above the quad seemed to take on the last gleam of sunlight. The air smelled thicker than I was used to, heavy with the scent of grass and leafiness and sour dishwater escaping from the open door of the kitchen. We passed the gym, and I felt the silence of the trees behind it, the same darkening woods that bordered our dorm; beyond it lay the town of Dumbarton and its souvenir shops and the lake I hadn't seen from the van and somewhere nearby the Turnblads' house itself, all lit up inside except for Chet's room.

That night before bed, I gave Chet "Infants' Masada" to read—the same copy, thorny with checkmarks, that I'd given Ms. Nowinski. Chet's expression as he flipped the pages was blank. If he recognized its brilliance, he was keeping it to himself. When he finished, he put the story down and gave me a funny look, as if I'd confessed to being a werewolf.

"I like it," he said unconvincingly. "Is it supposed to be realistic?"

"What do you mean?"

"I'm just wondering if a preemie would be able to break through an incubator," he said. "Even if it was mad."

My face turned hot. "I took some artistic license."

"Also, I think newborns are pretty much blind."

"It's a retelling of Jewish history."

"Oh," he said thoughtfully. "They're, like, symbolic?"

I nodded, too angry to speak. A musician—a trombonist, of all things. What did he know about literature? I asked for the story back and stuck it on my desk, folding it over to the last page so that Ms. Nowinski's grade was showing. Chet's trombone case stood in the corner like the foot of an elephant. Its presumptuous claim to the room pissed me off.

"Let's hear you play that thing," I said, pointing.

Chet walked over to the boom box on top of the bookshelf and slipped in a tape from his collection. Probably he wasn't talented enough to play without accompaniment. The music started with a sad horn and brush of drums, the slow bleed of a ballad. I waited for him to take his trombone out, but he stood there with his head cocked like a bird's.

"Aren't you going to play?" I said.

"This is the band I'm in," he said. "My solo's coming up."

I listened more carefully, wondering how the hell a trombone was going to fart its way into a ballad. The saxophone that had been playing feathered out and then there it was, the clumsy blat of a trombone, except that it wasn't clumsy at all but steady and beautiful and full of tenderness. It was like a walrus in mourning. Then the mournful sound built to something else, mounting slowly as if climbing a ladder, working up to a boozy swinging wail that seemed graceful and unhinged at the same time. Beneath the groans and snorts the melody was always there, holding on for dear life. I understood that this was talent. It might have been the first time I'd come face to face with it. When the song was over, I put my story in my desk and then went to brush my teeth, unable to look Chet in the eye.

That night I couldn't sleep. My sheets were a tangle of sweat, and the rotating fan that Chet had brought blew humid gusts of wind on my face. I kept thinking about Sylvana: the weekend before I left I'd convinced her to let me take her shirt off, and now the image that hung before me in the dark was the pale shivering secret of her breasts. The police were patrolling campus for the Dorm Room Prowler, and I could hear the intercom on a squad car squawking in the distance, warning students to keep their rooms locked. I was soaked with sweat, I couldn't get comfortable, I wanted to strip out of my skin and wring it like a towel. Above me, Chet's bunk was silent as a grave. I started to touch myself. I had no choice. I did it as quietly as I could, trying not to betray myself, slow as a dream I didn't want to disturb, and then I heard a sound above me too, a quiet rustling, and for a second I thought Chet had joined in—a weird queasy thrill rising in my chest—but then the rustling grew louder, a voice in the dark, the sound of a boy crying softly above me.

That first week at camp, aside from the mornings when I was in class and Chet was doing his music, we were pretty much inseparable. There was the sense that we'd met a long time ago, in a previous life, and had fallen into some old friendship we didn't need to begin. At lunch, we'd take our trays to an empty table far from the dragon blasts of the kitchen, where the walls were peeling paint and a steel fan blew strong as a gale over our heads, long threads of dust waving from it like seaweed, and wait patiently for prey. We liked the acting students the best, because they were generally not the sharpest pencils in the box. Chet and I would leaf through the phone book in our room beforehand and come armed with the most absurd names we could find.

"What did you think of Dallendoerfer's last film?"

"Dallendoerfer?"

"I've heard four people here tell me he's uninspired."

"Well, I don't know."

"Greatest actor of our generation. That's a tall order." Chet or I would lower our voices, as if ashamed of our sacrilege. "I mean, who would you choose? Dallendoerfer or Funkhouse? If you had to pick."

Amazingly, we'd hold off laughing till later, repeating the best responses to ourselves and brandishing them throughout the day to crack each other up. I loved making Chet laugh because his stern-looking face would open like a fist, his mouth so wide I could see the trembling pink loogie of his uvula. It was a look of total, flat-out joy.

He'd bray like a hyena. Certainly you would never guess that he cried himself to sleep. It was the same thing every night: the small sound you might mistake for something else until a human voice emerged, sniffling and helpless. I never mentioned it to Chet. Partly this was because it seemed like a private thing, and partly it was because I was making my own sounds I didn't want to talk about. I never mentioned that he cried, and he never mentioned that I jerked off. Somehow the two things had become weirdly linked in my mind.

The weekend after we arrived, Chet invited me to his house for dinner. We'd already had Sloppy Joes twice that week, and so I was happy to take him up on his offer. Also, I'd begun to romanticize him and wanted to see where he lived. In my imaginings, the house near the lake had turned into a backwoods trailer, presided over by an alcoholic dad, someplace where the redemptive genius of his trombone playing would save him from a life of petty crime. I'd already begun a novel about him for my creative writing class called *The Cry of the Trombone.* He let me use his bike, an old BMX, and led the way on his skateboard.

"My sister will be there too," Chet said, kicking up a hill.

"What?"

"She's my twin."

I stopped the BMX. "You have a twin?"

"She's a girl," he explained. "We're not identical."

I was disappointed: I'd assumed he was an only child, companionless except for his music. I was disappointed in the house as well. It was not a trailer at all but a normal-looking house on a leafy street, complete with painted shutters on the windows. A bit small, perhaps, but no smaller than the other places on the block. There was even a tree house perched in a big oak shading the lawn. We walked around the side of the porch and through Chet's overgrown backyard, past dandelion clocks as big as baby heads, and wiped our feet on a doormat that had a chipmunk eating an acorn on it. Beneath the chipmunk were the words WELCOME TO THE NUT HOUSE.

His mom greeted me with a hug. She smelled like chewing gum. Maybe it was the gum, but I was shocked by how young she looked. I could see Chet's face in hers, surprised to discover that it was not unattractive.

"Chet's told me so much about you," she said. "How's the Great American Novel coming?"

"Copacetically," I said.

"What?"

"Actually, it's more of an antinovel. I'm exposing the underbelly of the American dream." I glanced at Chet, who was staring at me. I had no idea why I was speaking like this.

"Wow. Sounds like it's really something." His mother smiled vaguely, then plucked a hank of red hair from her face. "You like meatloaf, I hope. I was going to make pork chops, but then I remembered about your, um, heritage."

She reached behind her waist and retied the apron she was wearing, tugging it more firmly around her breasts. I'm ashamed to say that I imagined her in nothing but this apron. After the surprise of Chet's mother, dinner itself was disappointing: I was hoping for something I could use for my novel, but Chet seemed to get along well with his parents and no dark, pitiable secrets were revealed. His father owned a landscaping company, a promising development, except he turned out to be a nice guy with excellent manners who not only approved of Chet's trombone playing but seemed to be well versed in jazz himself, asking him about the new Lee Morgan tune he was adding to his repertoire. As for Chet's sister, I still hadn't met her: she wasn't feeling well—"a little off," Chet's mom put it—and had confined herself to her room. Her mother insisted on setting a place for her in case she felt well enough to eat.

"I wish you wouldn't waste food," Chet's dad said, referring to the slice of meatloaf growing cold on her plate. "We can make her a new one if she's hungry."

"She might get her appetite back," Chet's mom said. "It's unpredictable."

"It's not a normal way to have dinner."

"Sure it is," she said brightly. She turned to me. "Jason, don't you do that for Seder? Put out an extra setting?"

"Seder?"

"I might have my holidays mixed up."

I nodded. Chet's dad frowned and continued his meal, glancing at the uneaten slice of meatloaf every now and then and averting his eyes. Finally he stood up in midchew and grabbed the dish and walked it to the kitchen, where he stuck it in the fridge. The screen door wheezed open, then snicked shut. Chet's mother stopped smiling and turned pink. I glanced at Chet, who was plowing through his dinner as if this were typical behavior.

"I think your sister would appreciate it if you said hello," Chet's mother said finally, once he'd finished. "I know she's missed you."

His sister's room was on the other side of the house, abutting the garage, but rather than knock on her door we walked through the backyard to surprise her at the window. I had the feeling Chet had done this before. The giant dandelions swayed in the breeze, parachutes shooting from them like sparks. The air was even muggier than before, and it smelled like rain. "He likes to go for walks after dinner" was all Chet said when I asked him where his dad had gone. When we reached his sister's window, Chet approached quietly and we stood there for a minute spying through the open curtains. She was lying in bed and watching TV. Surprisingly, her hair wasn't red but a beautiful sandy brown. It was curly, too, long coils hanging to her shoulders. Beside her, stationed on the bedside table, was some kind of intercom: a white box with a call button on it. The window was open, and I could smell the stuffy warmth of the room even in the rain-scented breeze, a smell like the sour head of a baby.

I waited for Chet to say hello, but he just stared at her without speaking. His face was pale and rigid and there was a strange smile on it that did not seem to have anything to do with smiling. I began to feel frightened. The longer he stood there, the weirder I felt. Someone screamed on the TV. Just when I thought he was going to say something Chet made a face, a terrible mean thing I've never seen before: he bared his clenched teeth and forced his tongue through them as slowly as he could. It was like watching something squeeze out of one of those Play-Doh machines. Then he turned and ran away, startling his sister, who looked up from the TV and saw me standing at her window. She switched the sound off and slid gently out of bed so that she was standing at the window too, right there in front of me.

"Are you Chet's friend?"

I nodded. She was wearing plaid pajamas that she seemed to have outgrown a little bit. Below the cuffs of her pants I could see her ankles, pale and bony, and the long, slender blades of her feet. Her toenails were painted purple.

"Chet ran away," I said stupidly.

She clutched the neck of her pajama top, as if she were cold. "Mom says he's regressed. It was her idea to send him to summer school."

"Are you sick?"

She looked away. "No. I just hate meatloaf."

"Me too," I lied.

She smiled. There was something about it—not the smile itself but the effort to keep it on her face—that seemed to make her unhappy. She shut her eyes. A breeze swept the yard and blew a flurry of dandelion seeds into her room, swirling them like the snow in a snow globe. One of them landed in her hair. I reached through the window and picked it from her curls. I handed the bit of fluff to her—I don't know why—and our fingers touched, gentle as ants.

"Thanks."

She blushed. My heart was pounding in my chest. A stronger wind gusted through the window and a corner of her pajama top flipped up, revealing a tattoo under her belly button. A cross, it looked like. She tugged her top back down. For a moment I couldn't speak.

"It's going to rain," I said. "You should close the window."

"I like to keep it open."

"Why?"

She looked at me, one eye squinched up. "In case of visitors."

I turned from her window and walked back through the giant dandelions toward the front yard. When I found Chet again, sitting on his porch, he refused to talk about his sister. He didn't mention the terrible face he'd made at her, and I didn't mention our fingers touching through the window. It was like it had never happened. We said goodbye to his parents and rode home, me on the skateboard this time. He biked fast, and I had to struggle to keep up. We mounted the last long hill before campus, the clock tower rising into view like the turret of a castle, darkened by rain that hadn't reached us yet, but I was panting too hard to appreciate it. Thunder, loud and exotic to me, rumbled nearby. When I caught up with Chet, he wouldn't meet my eye, gazing instead at the rain-blurred campus trapped, it seemed, at the bottom of a well.

"Copacetically," Chet said, when I asked him how he was doing.

Whatever had happened back at Chet's house—and whatever strange grudge he was holding against me—seemed forgotten the next day. We went back to our daily routine of meals and girl talk and conspiratorial ridicule, though something strange had entered our friendship, a kind of embarrassment I wasn't sure which of us was the source of. At night, in the sauna-like heat of our room, my fantasies about Sylvana were replaced by Chet's sister: the brown swish of her curls, the way the wind had pushed her pajama top up her stomach. The touch of her fingers that seemed now like a kiss. Mostly I thought about that cross below her belly button: how it tortured me, the image of that holy thing in such an unholy place! What kind of girl would get a tattoo like that? In my fantasies, I stepped through the window and ripped her pajama top open with both hands before pressing my lips to her stomach, following the cross's spine to her panties. We did it, in every way I could think up: in her bed, on the floor, in the backyard with dandelion seeds swirling around us. She was more experienced than me but not so experienced she would make me feel stupid, only grateful to be in her tutelage. We went at it all night and then I left at dawn before Chet's parents got up, before Chet himself was awake, sliding back into bed without anyone noticing.

Obviously, I did not share my fantasies with Chet. Instead, I continued to work on *The Cry of the Trombone*, adding a character modeled on Chet's sister. I named her Miranda. She was sexy and troubled and estranged from her twin brother, the trombone-playing protagonist, because of her religious conversion but also because she was in love with the protagonist's best friend, Blake. The best friend looked like me, except that he had a "rakish scar" under one eye and had lost his virginity at age ten to his depressed babysitter even though she was engaged to be married. We'd just read "The Country Husband" by John Cheever in my fiction-writing class, and it had made a deep impression on me, not just the troubled and beautiful Anne Murchison but the way that Cheever managed to make everything sound better than it was in real life, as if the thing he was describing had died somehow and he was speaking at its funeral. *The image of the girl seemed to put him into a relationship to the world that was mysterious and enthralling.* This was the sentence that I'd highlighted in neon yellow, because the story had done the same thing to me: put me into a relationship to the world that was mysterious and enthralling. It was what I wanted for *The Cry of the Trombone.* I didn't know if my novel was "enthralling" or not, but it did have a mystery: that expression on the protagonist's face when he saw Miranda through the window. It became, in my vision of the book, the clue to everything. Why did he hate her so much? What was the meaning of that hideous tongue squishing through his teeth, slow as butter? It was the first time I'd thought of writing this way, as the probing of a mystery. It had never occurred to me that there was the world you lived in and then the one you wrote about, lurking beneath the surface. When I showed the first chapter to my writing class, the teacher proclaimed it "ambitious."

"You might give it a bit more detail," Ethan, of the dolphiny smirk, said. We were walking back from class together. He was working on a trilogy about the life of Karl Marx, and I was impressed by the size of his vocabulary. If his characters were strolling up a hill, he'd use the word "gradient" instead. As for my novel, he'd said the first chapter was filled with "lapidary prose." I had no idea what "lapidary" meant, but I knew from the way he'd massaged the word on his tongue that it was a good thing. "Like the girl's blanket. What kind is it?"

"I don't know," I said. "It's just a blanket."

"Is it an afghan? Fleece? *Virgin* wool?" he said, winking.

I shrugged. It didn't seem important to the story, but he clearly knew more about writing than I did. "I never thought about it."

"Anyway, I like how it's a roman à clef," he said kindly.

"Thanks," I said. It sounded even better than an antinovel.

"I mean, the protagonist. He's so clearly your roommate Chet."

I shook my head, feigning bafflement.

"Come on! He has long red hair, and wears a Red Sox cap just like Chet does. Plus he's a trombone player."

"Well, he might have been an inspiration," I said, waving some no-see-ums away from my face. "Subconsciously."

"You're not worried about his *feelings,* I hope?"

I shook my head again. It hadn't occurred to me to worry. Anyway, I was still bitter about what Chet had said about "The Infants' Masada." We crossed the main quad, where some creative anachronists were dressed up as knights and rehearsing a swordfight while some girls in lace-up frocks swooned from the sideline.

"Real writers," Ethan insisted, "love sentences more than people." He stopped to toss the bangs from his eyes. "Tolstoy wrote about everyone he knew. He destroyed people's lives. But nobody wishes he'd been nicer, that *War and Peace* didn't exist."

I hadn't read *War and Peace* and had no opinions about it, but I liked thinking of myself as being exempt from the same rules as everyone else. At dinner, I sat with Ethan in the front of the dining hall, not far from the policeman standing by the door. They were still looking for the Dorm Room Prowler—recently a stereo had gone missing from Crofton, a couple of twelve-speeds from Trimble. Eventually, Chet found us and sat down with his tray. I could tell that he was surprised to see me eating with someone else, though he did his best to disguise the fact by digging into his breaded veal patty. I felt a tug of remorse. Ethan made me feel high on myself—like we were special people, anointed by talent—but I didn't particularly like being around him. I would have rather been hanging out with Chet in the corner, rolling our eyes at the kids in black and cracking ourselves up. Ethan started talking about the short stories we were reading for class, how "pedestrian" they seemed. Many of these stories—like "The Country Husband"—I had loved. "If there's anything that bores me to tears," he said, "it's domestic fiction."

"What kind of fiction do you like?" Chet said.

"Literature. That embraces the world."

"Like James Michener?"

Ethan snorted. "No! God. I said *literature*."

Something strange was happening: Chet blushed, and it was as if

I'd blushed too. It was like I was watching Ethan through Chet's eyes. I leaned over my plate, waiting for Chet to retaliate. That's what the protagonist in *The Cry of the Trombone* would have done. "What do you think of Lichtenberger then?" he would have said, nudging Blake under the table. "Is his best work behind him?" He would have set the bait and then pounced. There would have been revenge, humiliation, the thrill of confrontation. Watching Chet saw through his veal patty, I had a weird sense I could make this happen. When it didn't—when he just sat there, frowning at his plate—I was disappointed.

That evening, back in our room, I flipped through my teacher's copy of *The Cry of the Trombone* and read her comments. She seemed to agree with Ethan that the chapter lacked detail. *What does he look like?* she wrote on page two, then *What does he LOOK like?* on page five, and then on page eleven: *WHAT DOES HE LOOK LIKE?* I put down the manuscript and stared at Chet. He was sitting at his desk, listening to his headphones and leafing through a *Mad* magazine he'd brought from home. Absently, he tugged at one of his eyelids with two fingers, out and in, out and in, making a kind of squishy eyeball sound. I could hear these faint little clicks. I recognized the gesture somehow—must have seen him perform it before—but had never taken the time to notice it.

"Why are you staring at me?" he said finally, putting down his magazine.

I blushed. "I wasn't."

"Quit it. You're creeping me out."

That week, I dove into the next chapter of *The Cry of the Trom-*

bone, trying my best to be as detailed as possible. I wrote a scene in which the protagonist finds his mother crying in the kitchen because his father threw a glass ashtray at her head at a Christmas party. There's a winter storm watch, and the father, drunk, is passed out in the car. "I'm going to leave him out there till he freezes to death!" the mother says. The protagonist has to go pull his father out of the car himself. This was something that had happened to Sylvana in Colorado, before her parents' divorce, which I'd promised not to tell anybody. In fact, she'd made me take an oath. I felt a little sick about this, but I was supposed to write as if everyone I knew was dead. Even our teacher had said that, issuing it to us like a command: *Write as if everyone you know is dead.* At some point, surrounded by corpses, I began to refer to the protagonist of my novel as Chet; it was an accident at first—the name just slipped out—but he felt sturdier that way, more convincing, and I couldn't bring myself to change it back.

The problem was Miranda, Chet's sister. She wouldn't come to life. I couldn't figure out why she was lying in bed in the middle of the day, or—the central mystery, the book's dark heart—why Chet had made such an awful face at her. Finally I couldn't take it anymore and set down my pen in despair.

"When did your sister get that tattoo?" I asked.

"What are you talking about?" Chet was cleaning the mouthpiece of his trombone, which lay in pieces on his desk. Seeing it that way— in a sad mess of parts—made his talent seem even more implausible.

"You know. That cross on her stomach."

He stared at the mouthpiece, screwing it with a little brush shaped like a Christmas tree. "That's not a tattoo."

"What is it?"

"It's not a tattoo. She's sick."

"She told me she wasn't," I said, as if I knew more about his sister than he did.

"Are you soft in the head? She has neuroblastoma. It's for the radiation—to show them where to do it."

I blushed again, mortified at my own stupidity. I didn't know what neuroblastoma was, but it sounded bad.

"Why do you think I'm here?" Chet said. "My mom's on the road half the week, driving her to Dana-Farber."

He went back to cleaning his trombone, picking up a long metal swab and threading a rag through an eye at one end of it. I came over to help him, and he looked at me in surprise. I held the trombone slide—or half of it, at least—while he cleaned the inside of it. Then we did the other half, and I helped him put the twin U's of the slide back together again. I felt real affection for him, and sadness about his sister, but there was also a strange bubble of excitement in my chest. It had to do with the word "neuroblastoma," which floated in front of me as if on a page.

Later, lying in my bunk after Chet had gone to sleep—there were no sounds of crying, as if I'd forced him into silence—I felt the same bubble of excitement. My heart began to pound, buoyed by the dramatic possibilities of his sister's illness. A dying girl. Her brother's hatred. The struggles of a family beset by illness. I was trapped in a daze. This had never happened to me before, doing nothing but lying in bed. I had the feeling of being very close to something, something better than I was though it came from my own brain; if I leaned an inch further, I could touch it. If I didn't touch it soon, or try to, it would disappear.

I climbed out of bed and slipped on my clothes and shoes as quietly as possible. Then I lifted Chet's silver BMX Mongoose bike with twelve-inch mag wheels from its hook on the wall, setting it on the floor without so much as a clink, and wheeled it out the door. I hopped on Chet's Mongoose and began to ride. The whole campus seemed to be asleep, quiet except for the chirp of crickets, and as I passed the silent bell tower, lit up against the lonesome vault of the sky, I shivered with longing. I jumped the moonlit curb and then mounted the gradient toward Chet's house. I stopped at the top, staring at the dead-end streets of Dumbarton. Now, there is a certain kind of neighborhood one sees in small New England towns where each house has a TV playing during dinner, and the lawns look small and lonely in the fading light of dusk, and the thin spaces between the homes make you think of the thin, precious distance between you and death. Where the Turnblads called home was just such a neighborhood. Everything looked different in the dark, but I must have known my way well enough, because I coasted into town and turned on a familiar-looking street and soon the small house with its overgrown yard and shabby tree house loomed out of the dark, the curtains of its windows drawn, concealing the tragic spectacle within.

I sat there for a minute, waiting for my chest to stop heaving. Then I left the bike at the curb and unlatched the gate as quietly as I could and rounded the side of the house to the backyard, which was even more verdurous than I remembered it. Probably the Turnblads' lawn mower had broken and they had no money to replace it. The giant dandelion clocks, taller than they had been two weeks ago, towered over the grass. *Time, that subtle thief,* I thought. I crept through them and stopped in the middle of the yard. My face was saturated with sweat. At first I thought the back windows of the house were as dark as the front's, but then one of them flickered and changed color, and my heart palpitated. Chet's sister's room. I could hear the sound of a TV set wafting through the open window.

She'd left it open for me, like an appeal for love.

I crept through the dandelions. She was lying in bed with an umber Pendleton blanket made of 84 percent wool pulled up to her waist. I could smell it from here, a scent like sheep. Trepidatiously, I knocked on her window with my right hand. She did not seem surprised to see me. She muted the TV, then got up and hobbled to the window. She had deteriorated since I last saw her: she was losing her hair, and I could see the cruel ladder of her ribs through the pajama top she was wearing. The purple polish on her toenails, once so new and shiny, was old and chipped.

"I'm dying, Blake," she said angrily.

"I know."

"I lied to you before."

"Youth is a lie," I said.

She nodded, like the dandelion clocks in the breeze. I stared at one of them. A breeze picked up and blew all the seeds away.

"Why did Chet make a terrible face at you?" I asked at length.

"I don't know, Blake. Perhaps he blames me for our father, what he's had to become."

I wanted to say something true, even lapidary, but I didn't know what. "What has he become?"

"Shhhh," she said, covering her lips with a finger and pointing to the intercom with the pointer finger of her other hand.

Suddenly, I listened. There were voices wafting through it, a man's and a woman's. I realized with a shock that they were coming from another room. Had they forgotten the device was on? Chet's sister and I watched each other while the voices filled the room, unbeknownst to their owners.

Janet, I'm a landscaper.

Just three more bikes. They'll never suspect one of the campers' fathers.

Janet, I'm a landscaper. I'm not a thief.

Do you want her to see Christmas? Your own daughter?

I'll go to prison. What if they catch me?

They haven't yet.

She's just a girl, Janet! A girl! Can't we find a cheaper hospital?

Nothing's cheap in America. Especially dying.

The first thing was a note taped to the door of our dorm room: KLEPTO, it said, scrawled in Magic Marker. Then, while Chet and I were walking to the student lounge, I saw some creative anachronists dressed in breastplates and lacrosse gloves glance at Chet and whisper to each other. This was a few days after we'd workshopped the newest installment of *The Cry of the Trombone* in class. I didn't make the connection at first, but then it began to sink in: somehow, what I'd written for the book had turned into a rumor, a gossipy allegation, except it wasn't Chet's father who was the Dorm Room Prowler but Chet himself. He'd been stealing people's stuff and sneaking it back to his house. Since he was the only townie in the camp—as far as I knew—this wasn't so hard to believe. Where would anyone else put the bikes and stereos they'd plundered? It only made sense if it was someone who lived nearby. I wondered, in amazement, whether the police were going to knock on our door and ask to speak with him.

That evening, I went to dinner before Chet got back from Jazz Theory and sat with Ethan and a girl from our writing class who'd turned in a short story told from the perspective of a toaster. (Ethan had been scathing about it to me in private—a Pop-Tartist, he'd called her—so it surprised me when he praised her "experimental impulse" at dinner.) Chet didn't come up, but when I saw him enter the Commons, looking for a place to sit with his tray of turkey Tetrazzini, a current of electric silence spread through the tables. It was as if a celebrity had walked into the place. Chet didn't look up from the floor, which relieved me of the burden of waving him over. He sat by himself at an empty table, near the restrooms, where no one usually ate. The Bog Table, we called it. I could see some drama kids at the next table talking about him, leaning in so he couldn't hear what they said. I felt guilt, yes, but also something else. A lift of power. I'd caused this to happen. It was amazing to me, that some sentences I'd made up had wandered into the world and done anything at all—had exiled Chet to the Bog Table, while I was stuck having lunch with some people I didn't really like.

After dinner, I went to the Pop-Tartist's dorm, where they were throwing a birthday party for her RA. Chet was asleep in the top bunk when I got back to our room, and then again when I woke up the next day for class. I climbed the ladder to look at him, feeling as lonely as I'd felt all summer. His face in the depths of sleep looked dreamy and remote, like a stranger's. When I got home that afternoon, Chet was packing up his cassette tapes, pulling them from his bookcase and tossing them into a box without bothering to keep them alphabetized.

"What are you doing?" I said.

"Moving out."

"But camp isn't over for two more weeks."

"I'm moving home early. I can bike to campus."

The hair squirreling out the back of his Red Sox cap was greasy, as if he hadn't showered in a while. I watched him pack up his things. Chet ripped his heavy metal poster down without bothering to pry out the thumbtacks, leaving four little right triangles on the wall. When he started on his books, I knelt down to help him, yanking them from the bookcase and tossing them on top of his tapes.

"Do you think this is Hinkenbottom's best work?" I asked, holding up a copy of *Roget's Thesaurus*. I'd seen the name in a real estate ad and had been saving it for two days. He ignored me, folding up the flaps of the box. I went to put the thesaurus back and saw my laboriously typed copy of *The Cry of the Trombone,* Chapters 1–5, fanned out on Chet's desk. I felt sick inside. I wondered if Ethan's theory about "real writers" extended beyond geniuses. How good of a writer would you have to be? And how would you know if what you were writing was worth it—if people would remember you as a novelist or a jerk?

"I'm sorry I used your life," I said.

Chet laughed. "What do you know about my life?"

"I said I was sorry."

"What about *this*? Right now? Is it going to show up in your anti-novel?"

"Tolstoy wrote about everyone he knew."

"Tolstoy?" he said incredulously.

My eyes burned. I picked up *The Cry of the Trombone* and assembled it back into a pile, smacking it on Chet's desk.

"Ethan likes my writing," I said.

Chet laughed. "He says that to everybody. At least when they're around."

I'd begun to suspect this myself, which made me even angrier. Chet turned away and began to pack up his trombone, taking the slide apart and then kneeling to place it in the case as if it were God's gift to trombones. He laid the bell on top of it, cradling it like a sleeping baby. I wanted to hurl the precious thing out the window.

"At least I have friends," I said.

Chet looked at me. It occurred to me that he didn't really want to move back home, that he was waiting for me to tell him to stay. He'd had all morning to pack—Friday was his rehearsal day, no classes—but had waited for me to get home. All I had to do was say *Sorry* or *Please don't go home* or *You're the only kid I like here,* and he would sigh and pretend to give in and call his mother to tell her not to come. But I didn't. I turned my back and did something egregious. I began to *whistle.* "Walking on Sunshine," a song I knew he hated. Chet buckled his case and stood up.

"You're right," he said, hefting it with one hand. "I don't have any friends here."

Soon after Chet moved out, they caught the Dorm Room Prowler sneaking into Crofton Hall in the middle of the night. It was an ex-teacher, an artist from New York, who'd been fired for "inappropriate behavior." Apparently, he hadn't sold any of his plunder, but had been keeping it in a storage unit outside of town and sleeping there at night. There was some question as to whether he was a drug addict. The most amazing part was his name: Schuesslefahrt. I laughed when I heard, but without Chet there it wasn't nearly as funny.

The last week of camp, I found out Chet was playing a concert as part of his jazz class, and I went to the auditorium on the south side of campus to see it. Ethan and I went there together. There were eight people in the band—the Octamerous Octet, they called themselves—seven of whom were dressed like waiters in matching black shirts and pants. The eighth was Chet, wearing one of those ties with cartoon notes on it. Ethan found this very funny, nudging my ribs and smirking his dolphin smirk. The smirk had started to annoy me, but I forgot about it when the band began to play—forgot, in fact, that Ethan was even there. It was strange to see kids our age do something so well. They were fleet and telepathic, smooth as a machine, swinging in perfect sync before one of the horn players stepped forward for a blazing solo. If they'd unzipped their bodies and some men in pork pie hats had stepped out, I wouldn't have been too surprised. Each of the band members had written a song, which they introduced beforehand. When it was Chet's turn, he leaned into the microphone and spoke in a nervous voice, gripping his trombone with two hands. The song was called "Blastoma." The band launched into the theme, which was stark and brooding, the horns tiptoeing through broken glass. It was beautiful, in an eerie kind of way. Eventually Chet stepped forward for his solo, but when he put the trombone to his lips nothing came out. He just stood there without playing a note. Or at least I didn't hear one. Judging from the looks on everyone's faces, the fidgeting and nervous giggles, no one else heard one either.

Finally Chet put the trombone down and stepped back from the mic. He had not managed a sound, and yet when the theme returned he joined the rest of the horns without a hitch, his trombone pitched in the air like a cannon.

At the time, it seemed to me like a terrible thing, to have frozen up like that. I said this to Ethan, who joked that Chet's tie must have sucked up all the notes in the room. It never occurred to us—to *me*—that he hadn't played anything on purpose.

"Anyway," Ethan said, "no great loss."

"What do you mean?"

"I've seen him play before. At rehearsal." Ethan leaned into me, as if to let me in on a secret. "He's not untalented, but hopelessly prosaic."

Chet Turnblad. Of course, that wasn't his name. I just like the sound of it. *Chet Turnblad.* I've searched his real name on the Web, but nobody who resembles him comes up. So I'm forced to imagine it, his Facebook page: a picture of him with his two daughters, both redheads, smiling into the camera while their hair flames to one side in the wind. They're wearing hiking boots, perched atop some rocky peak somewhere. His face is sunburned, half-hidden by one of those big Viking beards. He's taken over his dad's business, which is called Evergreen Landscape Services. His older daughter, Cassie, is an honors student. He's founded the Dumbarton for Cancer Bike Tour in memory of his sister. As far as I can tell, he doesn't play music anymore. He doesn't look capable of laughing like a hyena or crying himself to sleep or making a grown man want to apologize, thirty years later, for his failures of imagination. He just looks like a guy. I can see him perfectly, the first gray flashes in his beard. Because I'm not writing as if he's dead. I'm writing as if he's alive.

I did run into him one last time, the day after camp ended. My parents had flown out to get me—looking tan and refreshed from their European travels—and we were walking around the quaint part of Dumbarton, where the old church overlooked the river. It was a beautiful day, seasoned with a pleasant funk from the brewery nearby, and you might have thought—despite the number of teenagers strolling around in all black—that no one living there could really be unhappy. Passing a sandwich shop, I looked in the window and saw Chet sitting there with his twin sister, just the two of them. She was slouched in a booth, not nearly as skinny as I'd imagined in my book, wearing one of those concert T-shirts with the long white sleeves. If she'd lost any hair, I couldn't tell from the sidewalk. They had food in front of them—soup, it looked like—but they weren't eating it. They were making faces at each other, flaring their nostrils and baring their teeth in gleeful configurations of ugliness. Some kind of game. The Ugliest Face, maybe, or I'm Scarier Than You. It had the intimacy of a joke, one of those things you dream up as kids and never outgrow. Chet's sister reached up and flipped her eyelids inside out, exposing little red half-suns of skin. Her lashes stuck straight up in the air. Chet burst out laughing. I ducked my head and continued down the street, before they could see me.

"So what did you learn in your writing class?" my father asked, and I recited a bunch of words: Show don't tell. Write what you know. Be patient—some stories take years and you never get them right.

HEAVENLAND

Kevin confronted the ExerSaucer sitting in his ex-girlfriend's kitchen. Two years they'd lived here together, cooking each other romantic meals and eating them at the little dinette table Charlotte had found at a yard sale, and now Kevin's place at the table had been usurped by this hideous plastic toy. It was only one of several additions to the kitchen they used to share: a chalkboard with a list of random groceries hung over the stove, and a harness that looked like one of those carnival swings dangled from the doorway. The fridge, once happy to hum its tune and leave it at that, was plastered with Christmas cards and magnetic toy gears and a magazine clipping of "The 12 Most Contaminated Vegetables." Kevin flipped a switch on one of the gears and all of them began to rotate in a noisy horological display that made him wish he'd never gotten out of bed. He blamed this feeling on the baby lying in Charlotte's lap. *Their* baby.

"You'll have to take him out for a walk," she explained, as if he were a nanny. She was sitting at the kitchen table breast-feeding Arrow, the name she'd saddled his poor son with for the rest of his life. Kevin couldn't help staring at Charlotte's ample breast. It was just his luck that as soon as they broke up for good, she would become Brigitte Bardot. "It's the only way he'll nap. If he's overtired, I'll never get him to sleep tonight."

"I've done this before," Kevin said.

"I'm just reminding you. You can be kind of a space cadet."

Kevin squinted at her, in the mock-serious way she used to like. "I like to think of myself as a space officer."

"Ha ha," Charlotte said. "That really makes me feel better."

"You would have thought it was funny. When it was just the two of us."

"Ho boy. The two of us. Don't let's get started."

Kevin watched Arrow suck Charlotte dry and tried to coax himself into a smile. He'd offered to babysit the boy twice last month. The idea was to show her he could be a father. And he'd done that, or at least given it a shot—at all events, he'd managed to get through the ordeal alive. So when Charlotte had called this morning, after her usual sitter had phoned in sick—after, Charlotte was sure to inform him, she'd exhausted all other options—Kevin had agreed to watch Arrow while she spent the afternoon at the movies. Outside of work, she hadn't had a minute to herself in seven months. This was what she'd told him. And so Kevin had forfeited his plans to go to one of Druvi's famous pool parties—a party, his friend had said, that would enlarge Kevin's feeble understanding of the word—in order to spend his Saturday cleaning shit off his son's scrotum. In the privacy of his apartment, it had seemed like a good way to win Charlotte back. He could win her back and the three of them would live here together and maybe Arrow would not screw up his life as disastrously as he'd assumed. How bad could it be? But now that Kevin was confronted with the boy himself, listening to Arrow's gluttonous smacks and anticipating the hours of spit-up and back pain and crushing boredom that lay ahead, the inscrutable moans exploding into tears, he couldn't help feeling like he'd made a serious mistake.

Charlotte removed Arrow from her body, stealthily slipping her shirt back into place while the child groaned in protest. She spoke into Arrow's ear, and Kevin felt a creak of jealousy. He'd seen her only six times since the breakup, but her face still managed to star in his dreams: her droopy eyes and Slavic dagger of a nose, so thin she couldn't keep sunglasses from sliding down it, never ceased to amaze him. Today she was wearing a T-shirt with a picture of a ball-peen hammer on it. She had that effortless L.A. cool, the Warholian confidence that could make tools seem glamorous. He missed her so much sometimes he had to inflict harm on himself—clip his fingernails too short—to get his mind on anything else.

Perhaps Charlotte saw something in his face, because her eyes softened. "How are you? Work's okay?"

"I liked it better when the kids were all stoned." He taught studio art at City College, a job he once described to people as a high-functioning nap, but the recession had considerably upped the caliber of his students. "It's my birthday on Thursday. I'm thinking of bringing in some pot brownies."

"Christ," Charlotte said. "Is it August already?"

"The big three five," he said, bitter she hadn't remembered. "Will you buy me a present?"

"If you promise never to say 'the big three five' again. Or anything like it."

119

"Maybe we could celebrate early. Like this afternoon? You could skip the movies and the three of us could, I don't know . . . drive up to the observatory."

She looked at him, and for a moment her gaze melted in a way he'd nearly forgotten about. She peered out the window. They used to stay up all night talking sometimes and then sit here at dawn to watch the parakeets raid the fig tree in the backyard. They'd come down all at once, a green parachute of birds. It had seemed—to Kevin at least, hoarse with love—like something in a dream.

"I see figs," he said, squinting at the tree. "Haven't the parakeets been here?"

She kept her face to the window. "They stopped coming a long time ago. Before Arrow was born."

"You know, if he's going to sleep anyway, we could just stay here. I could grab some wine at the corner store. He still naps for hours, right?"

"Oh, Kevin," she said, darkening. "You just summed up the whole *clunk* of the problem."

"What problem?"

She didn't answer, but Kevin suspected that he and the problem were one and the same. Charlotte glanced at his waist, dandling Arrow on one knee. "Are you living on gin and tonics?"

"What do you mean?"

"Your jeans are practically falling off."

"I've been painting all the time," he lied. "I forget to eat." He tightened his belt. "So what about it? My idea?"

Charlotte stood up with Arrow in her arms and leaned toward Kevin, her face hovering a foot or so from his own, as if debating whether to float in for a kiss. His heart quickened. He could see the coronas of her contact lenses. Her eyes were red as a stoner's: somehow, exhaustion had only added to their beauty. It wasn't until she leaned away again that he realized she'd been sniffing his breath. Kevin stepped back, as if from a punch. The wound was like that: physical. He peered at the spinning gears on the fridge so she wouldn't see his face.

"If you go to the park, don't forget the changing pad," she said, nuzzling Arrow's neck. "Last time he leaked through his diaper."

Arrow cried after Charlotte left, watching from the window as she drove off to meet her friends at the Vista Theatre—how many movies had she and Kevin seen there, tangled like teenagers?—but soon enough the boy put his head on Kevin's shoulder and began to blow raspberries. How quickly he resigned himself to loss. Kevin sniffed him uneasily, and the boy looked up at him with a smile. It was cute and invincible and filled Kevin with feelings he didn't want to have. Sometimes, before the tedium and diaper battles had inured him to it, Kevin would look at this smile and feel something unhitch in his chest, like a gate. He'd read an article about how Arrow was trying to mess with his brain, how its levels of oxytocin and prolactin shot through the roof whenever the kid squeezed off a smile. It was chemical warfare. If Kevin had had his way, his hormones would not be under siege. Arrow would not have a stupid name—or any name at all. Kevin and Charlotte would still be together, living in her comfortable apartment, making lunch together and then fucking against the gearless doors of the fridge.

Him or the baby. He'd had no choice but to give Charlotte the ultimatum, as soon as she'd decided—against all odds—to keep it. How could she blame him? He'd been up-front with her from day one, just as he'd assumed she'd been up-front with him when she'd told him, on their first date, that having kids was "a failure of the imagination." That was the moment he knew they were meant for each other. Charlotte had had her own dreams then—she'd wanted to make documentaries, had even spent a month in Idaho shooting footage of a doomsday cult. Her PR job at Ball Peen Films was just a way of paying the bills. Now, of course, she no longer had time to pursue her dreams; or rather, her dreams had changed, contracted, become as small and routine as everyone else's.

It had never seemed the slightest bit appealing to Kevin, this sudden and unnegotiable adjustment of one's purpose on earth. He'd watched some of his friends from art school get married and start talking in a different language, referring to "playdates" and "onesies" and "Bugaboos," as if they'd been hypnotized by a Smurf. Like Charlotte, they'd given up on their dreams of greatness and chosen to settle for a life of Costco memberships and bedtime angst and half-chewed Cheerios boogered to the floor. These friends who'd belonged to Marxist "clown collectives," who'd been in art-punk bands with names like Molotov Cock Tease, who'd staged performance pieces that involved reciting *Ulysses* to a medley of reaction shots from *The Oprah Winfrey Show*—these same New York friends had become unflappable and resigned, content to work office jobs and dress their toddlers in Ramones T-shirts. On the phone, Kevin would ask them if they'd seen the Jenny Saville exhibit, say, and they'd sigh or cluck their tongues, as if he didn't understand the first thing about their lives. *If only I had an hour like that to spare,* they'd say with a strange mix of envy and smugness. *You're so lucky to have time to paint.*

Except that Kevin wasn't painting. He hadn't been to the studio in a month. For a while he'd been making real progress, working on his L.A. Disaster! series, oils he'd been doing on triptych panels: the first triptych, called *The Big One,* depicted the earthquake ride at Universal Studios during an actual earthquake, so that you couldn't tell where the ride ended and the disaster began. He had a similar idea for the next one, involving a film set and a terrorist bombing. A gallery in Culver City had been interested—the owner had described the earthquake painting as "Condo meets Signorelli"—but Kevin had lost interest in the project once he'd moved out of Charlotte's apartment. The truth was, it bored him. When he settled down to work, all he could think about was Charlotte's face, the way she sucked the right corner of her lip into her mouth when she was lost in concentration.

Now he lifted the baby carrier from its peg in the closet and strapped it to his chest. The Björn, Charlotte called it. Clearly men in Sweden didn't mind carrying their babies around like chimps. He snapped the waist belt and then began the perilous procedure of inserting Arrow into his quiver without dropping the baby on his head. While he was struggling with the boy's leg, which refused to slide through its hole, his cell phone began to play its robotic bossa nova. It was Druvi, wanting to know why Kevin wasn't at his party.

"I'm babysitting."

"Jesus," Druvi said gravely. "Did you lose your job?"

"Of course not." Kevin tried to keep the phone from Arrow, who was reaching for it and starting to scream. "Stop, Arrow. Let go!"

"Whoa, what are you—working at a daycare center?"

"It's not a *job*," Kevin said. "I have a baby. Remember?"

"Of course I remember," Druvi said unconvincingly. He was the last of Kevin's heterosexual friends to resist fatherhood; he had avoided children, successfully, by insisting they didn't exist. "I was just screwing around. What's her name again?"

"His. Arrow."

There was a splash in the distance, and Druvi muffled his phone. He said something—"Wonderbra," it sounded like—and a woman's voice laughed. Kevin and Druvi had moved to L.A. together after grad school, deciding that staying in New York was too predictable a choice. All their favorite painters were Californian, and there was something about the weird mayonnaisey light of L.A. that appealed to them. Plus they'd both grown up in the Midwest and were attracted to the sun-cooked glamour; they'd partake in this glamour while subverting it from the inside, with old-fashioned artistry. It never crossed Kevin's mind that Druvi would get famous without him, painting people's toenails with his own blood, the kind of stunt art they used to make fun of.

"Bring the little tyke along," Druvi said. "Where are you?"

"At home," Kevin said, before catching his mistake. "Charlotte's, I mean."

"Right down the street!"

"I can't bring him to a party. Charlotte would never forgive me."

"Excuse me, but she's the one who chose the baby over you. Right? Or am I forgetting to misremember?" Kevin didn't respond. "Anyway, I want to show you what I'm working on. I'm using marbles like paint. Marbles! You've got to see what they do to the fucking light."

Kevin hung up the phone. Druvi had never cared much for Charlotte. Kevin had met her at one of Druvi's gallery openings, when his plasma pedicures and vampire paintings were just beginning to get noticed by the press, and Druvi's relentless drug-fueled pursuit of her over the course of the evening meant she grabbed the first bystander she could find to ward him off. Kevin was drunk enough—on champagne, on envy, on his own failure—to rescue her. When Druvi surprised his guests by handing out vodka shots laced with his own blood, one of his infamous party "provocations," Charlotte had not shrieked like some of the women there but said, casually, "I hope you taste better than you paint," which caused Druvi's smile to slide off his face like a pie.

"Am I really supposed to drink this?" she'd asked, after Druvi had left.

Kevin shrugged. "Last party he had bouncers brought in, then insisted that everyone wearing yellow be forcibly removed. He said yellow was a sign of mediocrity."

"Charming."

"Then there was the party before that, when he drilled a peephole in his bedroom wall and then hired some porn stars to screw in his bed."

"Did you look?"

"No. I plugged it up with a martini olive."

"Good boy," she said. Later, they'd gone out for a smoke and she'd bumped against Kevin's leg. Even now, thinking about it, he felt his heart swerve like a fish.

Outside Charlotte's window it was snowing ash, insectile particles that eddied in the breeze. The San Gabriels were on fire. Last week

Kevin had wipered the ash from his windshield and driven out to the Rose Bowl to take some pictures of the mushroom cloud of smoke pouring from the hills. He'd had the vague idea he would use them for the third triptych in his series. The air had been gauzed with smoke, enough to make his eyes sting, but what had impressed Kevin more than anything were the joggers puffing around the park nearby. Even the moms and dads at the playground had acted as if nothing was amiss, chasing their toddlers around the swings as they squealed with delight. Kevin had begun to wonder if the fire was actually a hallucination, cooked up by his own elaborate loneliness. The feeling stayed with him that night as he lay in his Glendale apartment, surrounded by dirty clothes and year-old boxes he'd yet to unpack, watching the fire blaze more convincingly on TV. He thought of the future he and Charlotte used to spin for themselves like a web—they'd talk about moving to the San Juan Islands once they'd made names for themselves, restoring an old ranch where they could work all day in peace, where they could grow old and quiet and alike—and felt for a moment like he couldn't breathe.

The pregnancy had been a freak thing; Charlotte had used the same diaphragm as always, the one that had done its job hundreds of times before. An easy job, really, the one it was put on earth to do. But whenever Kevin brought up the freakishness of her pregnancy, the unlikely odds, it only confirmed Charlotte's desire to have a child. She started saying crazy things, like the diaphragm must have failed for a reason. *I was meant to have this baby,* she told him several times, even though she didn't believe in such things and had once ridiculed Kevin's stepfather for describing himself as a "spiritual person."

If she was meant to have a baby, then surely Kevin was meant to go to museums when he wanted to and savor the detours of his own mind and not feel terminally exhausted. He was meant to listen to music as loudly as he chose, songs that didn't include the word "banana" in them. He was meant to paint his masterpiece, something that would put Druvi's stunt-art shenanigans to shame—or at least have time to die trying. He was meant to spend his birthdays with Charlotte, however many remained, and have her all to himself.

Now, feeling Arrow's weight in his shoulders, Kevin tried to walk inside the shade cast by the stucco dingbats along Rowena, worrying the baby's head might burn. The child insisted on pulling off his sunhat as if it were attacking him. Kevin felt a twang in his lower back every time he bent over to pick it up. Occasionally a woman would flash a weirdly flirtatious smile, and Kevin would lean down and kiss the top of Arrow's head, trying to impress her. When he felt actual tenderness welling up in him, he decided to stop. He walked under the spermy smell of a carob tree in bloom and then marched along the Rowena Reservoir, a meticulously landscaped pond with footpaths and tropical plants and geese making lovely rippled wakes in the water. It was a beautiful sight, but in true Southern Californian fashion you weren't allowed to enter it. A green fence with No Trespassing signs encircled the park. Kevin peered through the fence at the reservoir's sparkling cascades and jeering beauty, one more thing he couldn't touch.

He and Charlotte used to call the park Heavenland, joking about its pearly gates.

Kevin glanced down at Arrow: he was fast asleep in his carrier, hanging there limply in a gallows dangle. It was as good as Ambien, the Björn.

Kevin didn't admit to himself where he was going, even when he turned on Waverly and saw the parked cars and the dead pot-ted plants in front of Druvi's Spanish Colonial. The door was open, and he could hear the *unsk unsk unsk* of dance music coming from inside. The party was in full swing. He tucked Arrow's hat into his back pocket and stepped inside, confronted by a crowd of twenty-somethings in bathing suits and asymmetrical haircuts. The musty smell of pot smoke permeated the room. As far as Kevin could tell, there were no other children. He decided this was okay. It was cool and subversive to bring your baby to a party, and anyway Arrow was a virtuosic napper. He could sleep through an earthquake.

Kevin walked through the house, hunting for some people his own age, and ended up on the back porch squinting at the amoeboid blob of Druvi's swimming pool. A few people were standing in the shallow end, sipping drinks and wading through a film of ash. Druvi, however, was nowhere in sight. Kevin walked over to the giant cooler next to the barbecue, doing his best to fish out a beer without wak-ing Arrow. He turned around and was confronted by a woman in enormous glasses, who startled so much that they nearly slid off her face. Her nose was round and small as a bonbon. Like Charlotte's, it seemed ill-equipped to keep anything on her face.

"What's wrong?"

The woman pushed her glasses back up with one finger. "I didn't see your baby. Is he okay?"

"He's asleep."

"Are you sure?"

Kevin nodded.

"He looks kind of dead."

"He's not dead," Kevin insisted.

The woman did not seem convinced. She plucked the little umbrella out of her drink and took a swig. She was Asian American—Chinese, Kevin guessed—and was wearing a midriff-baring shirt and a humongous belt buckle shaped like an armadillo. Her waist bulged over the belt in a way that would have been easy to conceal with a longer shirt. Kevin found it refreshingly midwestern, this willingness to advertise your plumpness.

"I hate babies," the woman said.

"You do?"

"Yeah. They're just so . . . I don't know. Stupid."

"Well, their brains haven't developed yet."

"Exactly," she said.

Kevin was intrigued. He took an icy sip of beer, enjoying the ache it brought to his head. Why had he thought coming here was a bad idea? He was at a party, talking to a drunk woman in hipster glasses. Her name, incongruously, was Joyce.

"Are you one of those full-time dads?"

"No. I'm a professor." He paused. "Of art."

She laughed, revealing a mouthful of perfect teeth.

"Do you always laugh at people's professions?"

"I'm sorry. Just the way you said that. *Of art.*"

Kevin frowned. "What do you do?"

"I'm a lawyer. Of the law."

"Really?"

"You seem surprised."

"You don't look like a lawyer."

"Thank you," she said. "It's TV law. Contract negotiations. I don't usually dress this way at work." She finished her drink and then leaned down to grab a beer from the cooler; Kevin watched her shirt crawl up her back, feeling like a pervert with Arrow dangling between them. "What sort of art do you teach anyway?"

"Studio art. You know, life drawing and stuff."

"Are your students any good?"

Kevin shrugged. "Some of them can draw a mean dragon."

Joyce laughed. Her teeth were so large and white that they looked uncannily like dentures. The effect was somehow erotic.

"I also teach a class called Art and Controversy," Kevin said, hoping to impress her. He'd only taught the course once, several years ago, and it had been something of a disaster. He'd gotten drunk while grading papers and had written *Are you fucking kidding me?* in the margin of an essay preferring *Piss Christ* to Goya's *The Disasters of War*. "We read Susan Sontag's *Regarding the Pain of Others*. You know, what's deemed 'ethical' and what isn't."

"Like bringing your baby to a cocaine party."

Kevin straightened. "This is a cocaine party?"

"Well, there's cocaine. And it's a party. Though that last part is up for debate, since you're the second person I've met who's brought up Susan Sontag."

Kevin looked around for a place to put his empty bottle. In the end he put it back in the cooler and grabbed another beer, thinking of Charlotte's face—its smug blush of relief—after she'd sniffed his breath. How helpless she'd look if she could see him now. He chugged half the beer, enjoying himself. "I was thinking of inventing a hat that would double as, like, a tabletop. For your baby to wear when you're carrying him around. Sort of like a mortarboard. You could rest your drinks on it."

Joyce regarded him carefully. "You're not really a professor, are you?"

"No," Kevin lied. He felt strangely liberated.

"Can you get rid of that baby?" she asked.

"Of course not."

"Too bad."

Joyce reached into the purse dangling from her shoulder and pulled out a Ziploc bag, which she handed to him. Kevin held it up to his face. "What is this?"

"Its whatness is coke."

"No way," he said. "I can't."

"Come on, treat yourself. Some guy stuffed it in my purse before I could refuse. I've got a heart condition, actually—I might drop dead if I use it."

"Really?"

She shrugged. "If I did, you'd feel terrible for not taking it off my hands."

She smiled and then walked into the house. Kevin had no choice but to stick the gift in his pocket. What was he going to do, leave a baggie of coke by the crab dip? He could have found a wastebasket, of course, but it wasn't every day someone gave him drugs for free, and he had the vague idea he might save it for his birthday. He drained the beer in his hand before realizing that he'd forgotten to eat lunch. He was tipsy and front-heavy and his back ached from the burden of Arrow's weight. He felt like a pregnant man. He followed Joyce inside and then wandered into the kitchen, where he found Druvi wearing one of those old-fashioned striped bathing suits that straps over the shoulders. The ceiling fan made auroral reflections on his shaved head. He was bent over the counter, stirring the contents of a martini pitcher with a long silver spoon.

"Is this a cocaine party?" Kevin asked.

"Isn't that redundant?" Druvi said. He looked up from the pitcher and blinked. "Holy crack. When you said you were bringing the baby, you actually meant it."

"You told me to!"

"What do I know about parenting?" Druvi bent down to look at Arrow's face, which was sagging like a dead flower. "Is it safe to keep him in that knapsack?"

"It's a BabyBjörn."

Druvi blinked at Kevin, as if he'd sprouted a second head. "How's the work going?" he said finally.

"Horrendous. The kids, like, actually want to learn."

"I mean your *real* work. The disaster series."

Kevin looked at the door of Druvi's fridge, which was blank as a canvas. "Oh, it's great. Amazing. I've had a breakthrough, I think."

Druvi grinned. "You bastard. I could tell you were hiding something. You've got that glow." He took a sip from the martini pitcher and then added some vermouth. "You know, I told Colasanti from Regen Projects about you. That you were the great unsung painter of our time. He seemed interested in dropping by your studio."

Kevin nodded. He did not know what to do with Druvi's unshaken belief in him; somehow, it made him feel even worse. Even in grad school, Druvi had often claimed he was the one destined for greatness. One of Kevin's professors had gone so far as to tell him he had "alien vision." *Make it strange,* this professor was always exhorting the class, using Kevin's work as an example. It was this that Kevin wanted for his series, a strangeness, but everything he tried to paint seemed as dull and familiar, as uninspired, as his own life. That was the problem: the world had lost its strangeness. He felt like those joggers circling the Rose Bowl, unperturbed, while the sky burned around them. At least his students' work, their heavy-metal dragons, sparkled with weirdness.

"Why the hell won't you put your stuff online? I had to tell Colasanti you were a Luddite."

"I don't believe in JPEGs," Kevin said.

Druvi clapped a hand on his back. "Luckily you're just in time for the experiment. Only primitive technology involved."

He grabbed a vintage Polaroid camera off the counter and told Kevin to smile before snapping a picture of his face. The flash was blinding. The camera groaned digestively and then relieved itself of a photo, which brightened slow as daybreak into Kevin's grinning face. Druvi folded the Polaroid into a square before sticking it in a top hat stationed on the counter not far from the martini pitcher. The hat looked like something a magician would use. Kevin peeked inside and saw that it was filled with other folded-up pictures, fodder for Druvi's "experiment," though Kevin knew better than to ask what the experiment was going to be. There was nothing worse in Druvi's universe than a guest who failed to play along or had touchy notions of "common decency." At least with Arrow strapped to him, they wouldn't dare throw him in the pool. Smiling cryptically, Druvi handed Kevin a martini without bothering to ask him if he wanted it. It was typical of his assumptions regarding martinis. In any case, Kevin did.

While Druvi wheeled off to deliver drinks, Kevin left the kitchen and wandered into the living room to sip his martini. Milling about were the typical assortment of Druvi's friends: hipsters in grandfatherly hats; beautiful women as sleek as mermaids; fellow artists of the lumberjack glamour school, flaunting mustaches as if they'd bought them at the Ye Olde Mustache Shoppe in Mustacheland. A couple of the hipsters glanced at Kevin and Arrow and whispered to their companions. Kevin ducked down to peer at Arrow's face, where a worm of yellow snot was peeking from one nostril. At one point, before she'd fully converted to motherhood, Kevin had convinced Charlotte to get an abortion. They'd driven to a clinic in Glendale, where she'd seemed to melt into the couch, crying as if she were the only one in the room. Her nose ran but she made no effort to wipe it. He grabbed a Kleenex from the receptionist, thinking he would offer it to Charlotte, but at the last minute he leaned down and kissed her face instead. The tang of salt made him woozy for a second. And the kiss did something to Charlotte as well. As in a fairy tale, some magic spell was broken and Charlotte had looked up at him, harsh and blinking, as if realizing suddenly where she was.

The boy had escaped nothingness by a hair.

Kevin peered into his glass and realized he'd drunk half of his martini. He drained the rest in a single gulp, then made his way to the bathroom to take a leak, a challenge given the impediment of Arrow. He aimed wide of the mark at first but then quickly learned to use echolocation, gauging the frequency of the splash to make sure he was centered in front of the bowl. He zipped up as best he could and then leaned down to wash his hands, forced to take in the sight of Arrow's face in the mirror. His eyelids had the tiniest blue veins in them, like the honeycomb on a dragonfly's wings. Kevin felt a drunken wobble of love. He blamed this on the child. It was a biological conspiracy, meant to brainwash him into joining the Björn Agains. And if you weren't a good father, if you managed to resist these surges and hold on to your dreams, the Björn Agains believed you to be irresponsible, selfish, *afraid*. They'd gotten hold of Charlotte, of course, and this was how she thought of him now. She couldn't even remember his fucking birthday. Reaching under the Björn, Kevin wriggled the baggie of coke out of his pocket, careful not to wake Arrow in the process.

There was a problem. He couldn't lean down with Arrow dangling from his chest; it was physically impossible. And he couldn't put Arrow down, because the boy would almost certainly wake up and start crying and then he'd be at a party with a real live hungry baby, which would certainly be a buzzkill. Kevin looked around for a ledge, something high enough for him to prepare a line on. Nothing. He had no choice. He tapped the coke onto the palm of his hand, trying to make a neat and tidy line. The result looked like the vapor trail from an airplane. He lifted it to his nose and snorted it as best he could. Someone knocked on the bathroom door, and Kevin lurched forward to lock it. When he glanced back at his hands, he realized he'd spilled the coke from the bag. A surprising amount had snowed on Arrow's head, dusting the whorl of hair at the back of his scalp. The doorknob began to rattle. Kevin leaned down and snorted the coke from his son's head, trying to clean every speck.

Miraculously, Arrow didn't wake. Kevin washed his hands carefully and inspected the boy's face, which was peaceful and snow-free, in the mirror. He felt good. Scratch that: great. He'd just snorted coke off his son's head! How crazy and unbourgeois could you get! He squeezed past the line that had formed outside the bathroom, savoring the pleasant burn in his nose. His head was singing some private song to his legs. It was like those cartoons where someone dies and their shoes sprout wings to float them heavenward. Kevin floated toward the living room, hoping to find Druvi and tell him what he'd done. Instead he found some strangers he was dying to see. A man in a purple hoodie and sunglasses, like the Unabomber at a rave, smiled at him. His arm was draped over a woman with entertaining freckles.

"Aren't you worried about waking him?" the hooded man asked.

Kevin looked down at his fingers. He was drumming them on Arrow's head.

"How cute," the woman said, staring at Arrow's hair.

"Dandruff," Kevin said, brushing at the boy's hair with both hands, which made Arrow whimper and flop around in his sleep. Kevin began to bounce up and down in the tribal sleep dance he'd seen Charlotte perform at home. Remarkably, it worked. Kevin started to give a witty critique of an article he'd read in his dentist's office, one about combating dandruff with almond oil, but then found himself on a tangent about the night guard his dentist had prescribed him, which made him look like a boxer. "Anyway, I was reading this article and thinking, like, there's real war happening, in Afghanistan and Syria, and yet we're reading about combating dandruff. I mean it just sort of sums up America, doesn't it?"

The woman glanced at her boyfriend, then wrinkled her nose. "I think he needs to be changed."

"What?"

"He's got a diaper?"

Kevin, who had not brought the diaper bag with him, chose to ignore this and continued out to the pool. The sun sparkled on the water. Or maybe the water sparkled in the sun. Together they had a sparkling effect. The party was much more crowded than before, filled with human beings in delightful stages of undress. Kevin found himself exceptionally interested in their faces. Most animals' faces looked pretty much the same from birth to death, but not so people's. They covered some serious ground, especially in California. The face you had now was only one page of a swift and depressing story. Except it didn't depress Kevin. The narrative of his face was so completely at odds with the way he thought of himself, which hadn't changed since he was about sixteen, that he'd come to think of it as unauthorized. A fabrication.

He wasn't thinking these thoughts so much as finding ones that were already there. Like his brain was a cathedral of paintings—of frescoes—and he just had to look around.

He fetched a beer out of the cooler and then scanned the crowd of twenty-somethings who tragically believed him to be older than they were. Sometimes he fantasized about meeting Charlotte's double, someone who didn't know him yet but was filled with all the Charlottey things that made her unique. An unfeminine love of beer. A habit of slaughtering jokes when she tried to retell them. An uncontrollable desire to pick lint out of his belly button. A loathing of thank-you notes and a tendency to choke up during movie trailers and a wonderful way of spinning around midstep and continuing to walk backward when she said goodbye, all without breaking her stride. She had done this on their first date, and Kevin had been worried she might walk into a pole. He missed these goodbyes more than he could fathom.

But it was okay. He wasn't going to let Charlotte deep-six his high. And he was high, all right—no worries there. He orbited the pool on his winged shoes and ran into the lawyer named Joyce, who was sitting on the diving board by herself, texting someone on her iPhone. Kevin approached her. Joyce looked up from her phone, her eyes shifting between his face and Arrow's dangling limbs.

"You actually did a line."

"No, sir," Kevin said.

"Go ahead. Stop smiling." Kevin told himself to frown, but he could feel the breeze on his teeth. "I knew it."

"Well, you gave it to me!"

Kevin punched her shoulder, playfully, and she flinched. He wondered if he was out of control. He took a deep breath, forcing himself to stop bouncing.

"Is he supposed to sleep so long?" Joyce said, kneading her shoulder. "Maybe you should get him home to your wife."

"I'm not married."

"Too bad. You look like someone who could really benefit from some matrimony." She eyed Arrow nervously. Kevin looked at the boy's remarkable, edamame-size toes, realizing he'd lost one of his shoes. "You could always come back later, right? Without him. I'd rather not be responsible for, you know, anyone drowning."

Was this a proposition? It certainly seemed like one. But Charlotte wouldn't be home for an hour and a half. By that time, Kevin would be far into the cruel earthward stages of the drug.

"Have you seen Druvi's studio?" he asked, tilting his head toward the guesthouse behind the pool. "I know the secret way in."

Joyce seemed intrigued. Or at least Kevin chose to interpret the noise she made as a sign of interest. He grabbed her elbow and led her behind the guesthouse to the hidden door around back, where Druvi kept a key under a potted geranium, ready to enact his plan. Except that Kevin didn't have a plan. That was the thing. He felt so crisp and purposeful, his head was such a well-painted church, that he'd assumed one was in place. He only knew that Druvi kept a futon in his studio for taking naps. Coincidentally, Kevin had a napping child. The important thing, he reminded himself, was to show Joyce that he and Arrow weren't physically attached.

He opened the door upon a jumble of boxes and scavenged junk and an enormous canvas propped against one wall, shimmering, Kevin realized, with thousands of marbles. Amid the toxic smell of glue was the stink of gym clothes discarded under a punching bag in the corner. While Joyce inspected the painting, Kevin wove through open boxes of marbles to the futon by the window, then went about trying to extract Arrow from the Björn without waking him up. The idea was to move him from one cloud to the next. As he'd seen Charlotte do, Kevin lay on the futon and then undid the various snaps and latches, Houdini-ing himself from the whole contraption. But when he tried to slide the Björn out from under Arrow, worried he might entangle himself, the boy woke up and screamed in outrage, screwing up his face as if he were trying to flatten his eyeballs. There was a smell, too, befitting his fury. Kevin shushed the boy desperately, patting him on the butt as Charlotte had instructed him once. A surprisingly hard pat, somewhere on the spectrum of spank. To Kevin's surprise, the drubbing seemed to work: the boy's eyes slipped shut again, his breathing deepening to a steady rasp.

"I spanked him back to sleep," Kevin whispered to Joyce, who was still staring at Druvi's painting. He felt a weird tingle of pride.

"You generally do that? Punish him for being awake?" She poked her glasses up, squinting at the painting again. "I like how the marbles seem abstract at first. It's like a Chuck Close. You have to get some distance to see it."

Kevin frowned. "Actually, I'm not sure it's his best work."

She smiled. "Is that right?"

"I'm a big fan of his stuff, don't get me wrong, but another part of me thinks it's a bit, I don't know . . . gimmicky. I mean, a real artist shouldn't rely on one-liners. Charlotte calls him the King of Schlock Value."

"Charlotte," she said, nodding.

There was something about her face, its jealous squinch, that aroused him. He had a mysterious urge to make love to her against Druvi's painting. Instead, he took her by the hand and led her into the adjoining bathroom, where a pile of bald Barbie dolls greeted them from the counter. In the sink was a raft of hair, floating in what smelled like Easter egg dye. This whiff of industriousness made Kevin feel even more desperate. He slipped his hand under Joyce's shirt. She did not seem surprised. He had not touched a woman in a long time, and the smoothness of her skin made his throat dry up. She took off her glasses and laid them by the Barbies. Trembling like a teenager, Kevin pulled off her shirt and then fell to his knees and began to kiss his way down the fleshy brown turnpike of her stomach, which tasted deliciously of sweat. Her skin was warm on his lips. When he got to her waist, however, he paused. There was something in her belly button. He dug it out with his fingernail: a piece of lint. He stood up suddenly, then sat down on the toilet and closed his eyes. He felt sick. When he looked up again, he saw Joyce staring at him in her bra, her eyes damp with something he'd missed until that moment. A G-rated sorrow.

"What would Charlotte call *that*?" Joyce asked, looking away. She covered her stomach with one arm.

"Pitiful," he said, clearing his throat.

She slipped her glasses back on. "So you're not a professor. And you're definitely not a lover. What else aren't you, in case I make a third mistake?"

Joyce put on her shirt and left, the door to the guesthouse banging behind her. Kevin did not know how long he stayed in the bathroom. Heaped and hairless, the Barbies on the counter looked like a war crime. He went back into Druvi's studio and turned to the futon by the window, but Arrow wasn't there.

Kevin's heart stopped. He called the boy's name, scouring the room, checking behind the enormous painting and in the heap of gym clothes and around the steel hospital desk covered in sketches and magazines and costume wigs. "Fuck," he said, trying to stay calm. He threw open the window curtains: nothing. Could he have left the door open? It was closed now, adorned with a mirror that startled Kevin with his own ghost. He yelled Arrow's name again. The punching bag in the corner swung gently on its chain, twirling back and forth. Kevin jogged toward it and rounded an easel in the middle of the studio and almost tripped over a box, then caught his balance and saw Arrow frozen midcrawl in the narrow strip of room that had been blocked from view. He was studying something on the floor. Kevin let out a breath. Arrow fell to one elbow, and then lifted his head, and then Kevin saw that his face had turned a deep and stupendous blue. His first thought was that his son had transformed himself like a chameleon. But then he saw his bulging eyes, the awful terror of his face. Kevin ran to him and swept him up and felt how silent he was, the boy's mouth making no sound at all, gaping like a yawn that wouldn't stop, and Kevin hung him over his arm and began to pound his back, smacking him below the shoulder blades, hard enough to break something but there was that same eerie silence, no sound to the smacks, only Kevin pleading with the boy to breathe, and when nothing emerged from Arrow's mouth he held him around the waist and reached into his throat, clawing with one finger, shoving in as far as he could before touching something hard, a smooth and tumorous thing, and Kevin forced his hand even farther, scared he might tear the boy's throat, lodging the thing deeper before managing to hook his finger around it and pulling it out with the *sluck* of a cork. A marble. It bounced on the floor and dribbled away. Arrow gasped and sputtered, his neck pushed out like a turtle's, as if he were caught under a fence. It was like watching a death in reverse. Kevin felt the tininess of his heaving lungs. The boy's face faded to scarlet, then red, then back to its usual bologna pink.

Kevin stood there clutching him. He didn't dare move. His heart pounded in his ears. He had no sense of time passing, only that Arrow was very still, crying in his arms. On the far wall was Druvi's marble painting, glowing in the sunlight from the window. It was only after staring at it for a long time that Kevin realized Joyce was right, that the different-colored marbles formed something he recognized, something real and painstaking and gorgeous: a mountain in flames, heaving up an enormous cloud of smoke.

Kevin did not stop to get the Björn or pause in any way as he left the studio and rounded the guesthouse, Arrow quiet now in his arms. The pool was strangely deserted, waves plashing against the side as if a sea serpent was swimming down there below the ash. The music had stopped or was so quiet that Kevin couldn't hear it. He burrowed through the guests spilling out of the house and found Druvi in the kitchen, talking to a group of admirers by the bar. Kevin rushed up to him and began to tell him what had happened, but Druvi did not turn in his direction or say hello. Perhaps Kevin was imagining his own voice. He cleared his throat and addressed Druvi by name, loudly this time, but his old friend continued to ignore him. What's more, the people he was talking to refused to acknowledge him as well. Clutching Arrow in one arm, Kevin grabbed Druvi's shoulder and shook it, but Druvi did not turn or even lift his shoulder. It was as if Kevin's hand did not exist. An ink-squirt of fear blossomed in his stomach. He walked away and approached a couple he recognized from another one of Druvi's parties, babbling at them, feeling himself close to tears, but they stared right through him, sipping their martinis. The fear in Kevin's stomach hardened into dread. On his way to the sink for a glass of water, he saw Joyce filling a paper plate with hors d'oeuvres. He signaled to her, relieved, but she did not return his gesture. "Hey!" he said, stepping in front of her. She stared at her plate, inspecting a wedge of spanakopita before popping the whole thing in her mouth. She did the same thing with a crab cake. Kevin batted the plate from her hands. Hors d'oeuvres rained to the ground. Without looking at him, she grabbed another plate and began to fill it with a new assortment of food, crab cakes and bruschetta and little pink tongues of sashimi.

Kevin left the party and walked outside, clutching Arrow to his chest. The ash had disappeared from the sky, along with the smell of smoke, and the jacaranda trees along St. George seemed to breathe in the gathering dusk. There was no shadow at his feet, and the rustle of the trees covered up the sound of his steps. Kevin pulled Arrow's hat from his back pocket and recalled the top hat stuffed with Polaroids. He'd been the victim of one of Druvi's pranks. The realization did nothing to unknot the dread in his stomach. The breeze had turned cool and nocturnal, and he tucked Arrow into the crook of his arm. He remembered the night he'd gone to the hospital after Arrow was born, the first time he'd seen Charlotte since he moved out, how startled he was to see the ugly little creature, red as a kidney bean, asleep in her arms. Its umbilical stub had looked like one of those firecrackers that turn into a snake of ash. But it wasn't the baby's ugliness that impressed him the most. It was the smile on Charlotte's face: so remote and lovely it seemed, like something under glass.

A sprinkler turned on suddenly, spraying Kevin's shoes, but Arrow did not lift his head from Kevin's chest. Perhaps the boy had already forgotten about it—the marble. It would be Kevin's secret, something to take to the grave.

Passing the Rowena Reservoir, its immaculate pond and picture-book family of geese, Kevin noticed that the service gate was open. No one was guarding it. He ignored the No Trespassing sign and slipped through the gate, sneaking past a small brick building that looked like it might house a shed or a bathroom and into the deserted park with its pristine palms and quaint little waterfall tinkling down some rocks. He did not see the landscaper anywhere, only his pickup truck, and so he went down to the water and walked along the perfectly groomed footpath. Even though it hadn't rained for months, there were no footprints of any kind. The pond smelled of ammonia and something else: beach towels left in the car. Kevin stopped by a palm tree near the waterfall, where Arrow could get a clear view of the geese. He just wanted to sit down for a few minutes and relax. And so he did that, and leaned against the tree, positioning himself so Arrow could see the water.

He had not, like Druvi, made anything of his limited talents. The fantasy that he and Charlotte would get back together again was just that: a fantasy. Perhaps her choice—to break up, to have Arrow without him—had not been only about the baby.

Kevin touched Arrow's shoeless foot, which was cold as ice. He tugged off his own sneaker and removed his sock and then put it on Arrow's foot. The sock was too big to do much good, so he pulled it up to the boy's crotch like a leg warmer.

A disaster series! Why had he thought he knew anything about disaster?

Arrow lifted his head and scatted in his tuneful gibberish, pointing at the water. He was still and wide-eyed, mesmerized by the geese floating nearby. What did the birds look like to a baby? Kevin could only imagine. The boy could have died, and now these two enormous birds were swimming toward him, connected by a string of yellow goslings. Their necks swiveled back and forth, like periscopes. The lead goose swerved to avoid a leaf, and the gold string wriggled but didn't break. Beyond the geese, on the other side of the pond, was a cactus with big white flowers blooming from it. It seemed to Kevin that the flowers were opening as he watched. Was this possible? The flowers, the long-necked geese, the fringes on the palm leaves flaming in the wind—for a moment all of it seemed strange to him, as new as the child in his lap. One of the geese stopped and began to clean its feathers, burying its beak inside a wing. Arrow watched, transfixed. Perhaps he had never seen a goose before. Imagine all the other things he hadn't seen, the amazements in store, glimmers of a world that had not yet started to betray him.

"Geese," Kevin said. He felt a peculiar urge to name things. He wanted to stab each heartbreaking bit of the world, hold it up for the boy on a stick. A man's voice startled him from behind—*Yo! Hey! Dad with the kid!*—and he turned to see who was calling him.

TROJAN WHORES HATE YOU BACK

They reached the top of the Grapevine and then puttered over Tejon Pass, beginning their roller-coaster descent into Los Angeles, that vast sedimentary basin where everything comes to rest. You couldn't coast down the 5 without imagining you were heading down its drain. Even so, Alistair felt the old loop the loop of excitement. He gripped the steering wheel with one hand, trying to ignore the bursitis in his shoulder. He shouldn't have been driving, but it was his van—his MasterCard, in fact, bankrolling the whole reunion tour—so he could endanger his bandmates if he felt like it. And wasn't pissing on danger what Trojan Whores were all about?

A food truck drifted into his lane, straddling the dotted line so that Alistair couldn't pass. He could not lift his arm enough to honk. "Frozen shoulder," his doctor called it, which did nothing to describe the pain.

"Get out of the way, Pussy Kitchen!"

"Did you just say 'Pussy Kitchen'?" Glenn asked. He was slumped in the passenger seat, noodling on the unplugged Jaguar in his lap.

147

"Maybe."

Glenn nodded in approval. "I smell a hit."

He improvised a riff on the Jag, a Crampsy bit of staccato picking. The guy still had it. He was some kind of genius—could pull riffs out of the air like he was picking cherries. Alistair grinned but couldn't help thinking, as he had for the past two weeks, that his old friend's heart wasn't in it. Sometimes he glanced at Glenn's face and kind of, you know, wondered where he'd gone. His eyes bulged slightly, and his head looked sort of oblong without his old snowdrift of a pompadour, and there was the vague sense that he was making a face at you even when he wasn't. Somehow he'd gone from being the heartthrob poster boy of Trojan Whores to someone you might avoid sitting next to on the bus. Behind him, in the backseat, Vladimir was perched on his hemorrhoid pillow, an inflatable blue donut he carried around with him wherever he went. He'd developed one of those things on his eyelid that old people get, like the stalk of a miniature third eye. And what was he wearing? A windbreaker? Blue linen shorts? If you saw him cruising the links in a golf cart, you wouldn't blink.

At least Andy, zonked against the opposite window, still looked like himself: a bit pickled around the eyes, but more or less the same Andy he'd been in 1982. Maybe the secret was sleep. The only thing that could truly rouse him was a drum kit.

Alistair focused on the road, trying to ignore the smell of rat shit stinking up the van and wondering if the scratching sounds coming from the back were real or imaginary. The rats were for Vladimir's pet python, Stew. He'd insisted on bringing it along on the road. No doubt he'd had some trouble finding a snake sitter. Watching Stew eat a live rat was one of those life-altering experiences Alistair had not known to avoid until it was too late. The thing got fed once a week, which meant it was due to be fed today—as Vladimir kept reminding them from the backseat.

"I'm not playing any new songs," Vladimir said now from atop his donut. He looked, in the rearview mirror, like he was riding on a booster seat.

"Vlad the Complainer speaks," Alistair said.

"I'm not a complainer. I'm simply protecting our brand."

Glenn stopped playing his guitar. "Did you hear that? He just called the Whores a 'brand.'"

"Cut the horseshit," Vladimir said. "You need the money as much as I do. I've got a thirty-year mortgage and two kids going to college. Not to mention medical expenses."

"Funny he doesn't mention his weed habit."

"Like I said: medical expenses." Vladimir fished his vaporizer from the pocket of his windbreaker and took a hit, then cracked his window to blow out the mist. He was the only person Alistair knew with a medical marijuana prescription for hemorrhoids. "Poor Stew. Can't you drive any faster? He strikes at me if he's hungry."

"I know how he feels," Glenn said, turning up the radio.

"Physic?" Vladimir said sweetly, offering his vaporizer to Glenn.

"I'm stoned on God."

Vladimir laughed. Alistair wanted to defend Glenn and his God trip, but the truth was he didn't understand it himself. How could anyone belt out the chorus to "Immaculate Cuntception" every night and then unwind with the Holy Bible before bed? As far as Alistair could tell, Glenn had been on Genesis 13 since Texas. He knew this because he and Glenn had been sharing hotel rooms. If he wasn't

kicking it with the Word, the guy was reading a book of Chinese proverbs his sponsor had given him, trying to access his inner wisdom.
Last night, Alistair had watched him poring over some proverbs in
the next bed, lips moving the way they used to when he was writing
a song, and felt inexplicably jealous. He wanted to ask Glenn about
it—about the proverbs, the Bible business, what killer drug God was
dealing to make him so damn *fulfilled*—but was afraid he'd take it the
wrong way.

"Does Naya know we're playing the Wiltern?" Glenn asked.

"She listens to Nina Simone. It doesn't mean anything to her,"
Alistair said. "Anyway, she's leaving me."

"You don't know that."

"Well, she did say that being married to me was like being married
to one of those frogs that eats its own skin."

"What does that mean?"

Alistair shrugged. "I guess it's a metaphor."

"There's an old Chinese proverb: 'If I keep a green bough in my
heart, the singing bird will come.'"

"Also, she's looking for an apartment," Alistair said.

Something lurched in his chest, admitting this. If his heart were a
bird, it was very sick. A motorcycle—a Ninja, or a Samurai, or some
other Asiatic warrior—swerved into the next lane. The guy on the
motorcycle was dressed up like a clown, red afro billowing from the
bottom of his helmet. He had the gigantic bow tie and everything.
The motorcycle shot ahead, slaloming through traffic.

"Did you see that clown?"

Glenn glanced up from his guitar. "Judge not," he said judgmen-
tally, "that you be not judged."

They passed the Magic Mountain tower, poking from the earth like a giant red nail, and entered the fathomless outskirts of L.A. Then something miraculous happened. A Trojan Whores song came on the radio. "Curb Appeal." Alistair turned it up, and for a moment none of them spoke, listening to the young and desperate sounds rattling the speakers. Vladimir shook Andy awake. He stayed that way, blinking at the stereo. Never had they heard a song of theirs on the radio. There'd been rumors, of course, passed along by fans—but they'd never been able to confirm them. Glenn, proverbless, let his guitar slide to his lap. Alistair chose to believe he was moved. The DJ came on and gave them a shout—"Last chance to see Trojan Whores, tomorrow night at the Wiltern"—and Alistair's eyes fogged up. The whole thing was supposed to be a lark, a prank: two kids out for blood and pussy. How had it become the most important thing that had ever happened to him?

In the city, Alistair parked in front of an inauspicious building— "Lamebrain Productions," it said on the front—and tried to calm his nerves. He wished their gig at the Wiltern was tonight. He'd come to think of it, dangerously, as the passport to their future. For years, Alistair had been opposed to getting the Whores back together. He didn't particularly want to die before he got old—just didn't want to have to sing songs with names like "Immaculate Cuntception" in public. But then something had happened. He'd been walking to the BART station on his way to work one morning when he saw an enormous brown hawk swoop down and grab a squirrel that was high-wiring across a power line. One moment the squirrel was there, its long tail contrailing behind it; the next it was gone. It was a gorgeous day, the sun painting the windows of the Victorians on Twenty-fourth. People strode down the sidewalk with their eyes glued to their cell phones, thumbs dancing like flames. Alistair turned around and went home. He tracked down Glenn's number and found him in L.A., living in a friend's garage, out of rehab and hoofing it to NA meetings twice a week, so broke he had one of those disposable Walmart phones. It was for Glenn, Alistair told his wife, that he quit his job at Sunset Fire Protection and proposed getting the Whores back together. Glenn, who if he'd only died young would be as famous as Sid Vicious, but was a burned-out fatso without a penny to his name or any discernible vocational skills besides finding veins.

Burned-out, but not forgotten. Improbably, the reissue of *Trojan Whores Hate You Back* had found a tribe of *Pitchfork* readers who hadn't even been born the first time it came out. Three nights ago, at the Crescent Ballroom in Phoenix, Alistair had been amazed to look up and see two teenage girls in the front row, shouting along to "Sex Is Boring." They knew the words better than he did. According to Glenn, who still had some connections, Merge was interested in a new album. ("Intrigued by the idea," was how they'd put it on the phone.) Mac himself was coming to the show tomorrow night, to find out how intrigued they should be.

"We're doing a talk show in a mini-mall?" Vladimir asked from the backseat.

"It's a Web thing," Glenn said. "Our chance to go viral."

He smiled at them, as if the Whores' future were in his pocket. He'd insisted they didn't need a manager—that he could DIY a tour better than some "corporate douche"—and maybe he was right: Trojan Whores were on the radio. And yet there was something about his

152

enthusiasm that seemed, well, *contractual,* as if he were freeing himself of a debt.

Alistair had some trouble getting out of the van unassisted. Meaning: he couldn't. His shoulder, while not actually frozen, was definitely experiencing a wintry mix. Glenn came over and hugged him to the ground.

"Shit!" Vladimir said, unloading the van.

"What's the matter?"

"Stew! He's not in his cage!" He turned on them savagely. "Who forgot to fucking pin the top back on?"

"Wasn't me," Glenn said, in a way that made it clear that it was. He'd been poking the snake while Vladimir was in the Conoco bathroom, trying to get it to come out of its hide box. Vladimir began throwing drum stands and distortion pedals into the street. Alistair put his good arm around Glenn, watching their bass player freak. It was like old times.

"You mean there's a fucking loose python in the van?" he said happily.

Glenn whistled into the open doors as if Stew were a dog, calling him by name, which made Alistair laugh. He had not put his arm around Glenn in thirty years. Of course, there'd been a time—say, in '85 or '86, after Trojan Whores had been at it for five years—when a loose python in the van would have seemed like one more stop on the Tragical Misery Tour, as Vladimir had dubbed their life. Rubberneckers started coming to the shows and waiting for them to implode. Once, for a reason he could not afterward recall, Alistair snapped in the middle of one of Glenn's strung-out solos and attacked him with the mic, beating him in the face and screaming, "I'll shrink your

153

fucking head!" over and over, until it achieved a kind of contrapuntal rhythm to the drums. At night, sleeping on some crazy addict's couch, Alistair would dream of his childhood bed in Claremont, where he and Glenn had grown up. People went jogging there and listened to Springsteen and had trampolines on their lawns.

And so he'd left one day without telling Glenn: moved out of their apartment in East Hollywood, taking nothing but his records and whatever clothes he could fit into his dad's old army duffel. It had felt like an emergency. *I want a normal life*, he'd written, skewering the note on the turntable, where he knew Glenn would see it whenever he woke up from his drunken coma. And that's what he'd found. He'd moved to San Francisco, framed buildings for a while, then took some computer classes and got a job designing fire sprinkler systems. The job bored him, in a not-unpleasant way, and the smart-ass camaraderie of the other designers reminded him a bit of being in a band. He bought a tiny house in the Mission, before Silicon Valley colonized it. He dated a chain of women—volatile weather systems, given to dark silent prayers to the self—and wondered if he was destined to die alone. Then he met Naya. She had a master's degree and worked as a therapist for at-risk youth. Even her name sounded healthy, like a karate chop. She'd grown up in Georgia and had an enchanting disregard for syllables. ("CoCola," she ordered on their first date, and he was smitten.) They went to museums and fed the ducks at the park and hiked through trees as old as cathedrals. They were ambivalent enough about kids that after trying for a year they decided to stop. Even after sixteen years of marriage, they had regular, loving, secret-universe sex. He was happy enough, lost in the moment—but Happiness eluded him. He couldn't help feeling like there was something else he needed to do. It reminded him of that old Steven Wright joke: *I bought some powdered water, but I don't know what to add.*

And so he found himself missing Glenn, those first years after they'd moved to Hollywood, fresh out of high school and pissed off at anything that wasn't a guitar. The world was an enemy country, so they could do whatever they wanted. Once, Alistair had put his head through a pane of glass. One of those miraculous trucks with sheets of glass strapped all around it, just sitting there by the curb at 3:00 A.M. and pulsing with the lights of the Strip, pink and purple and fuck knows what else—the city was full of such things, dreams masquerading as objects. Back then a truck or a lost shoe could break your heart. Glenn had dared him to do it, half-jokingly—*If you're so fucking punk, then stick your head through that piece of glass*—and he'd closed his eyes and run at it like a football player and rammed his head through without a scratch, the thing crashing wavelike over his back. If not for his leather jacket, he might have ended up in the ER. The truth was he'd expected to die, but was too happy to care. It was the first he'd ever heard of it—trying to commit suicide out of joy.

That's what he'd wanted in getting the Whores back together. That feeling of possibility, that his heart was an open perch.

Now, after popping enough Advil to ulcerate his stomach, Alistair rang the doorbell of Lamebrain Productions. A chick in a Black Flag T-shirt greeted him at the entrance. She couldn't have been more than nineteen, betrayed by a pimple on her forehead. Her concealer had turned it into a beige growth. Did these beautiful girls really listen to Black Flag, charmed by the lyrics to "Slip It In"?

"Can I help you, sir?" she said to Alistair.

The "sir" lanced his heart. She squinted at the minivan, where

Vladimir was standing among the rubble of Andy's drum kit, looking like he might cry. Glenn smiled at her, lifting a Jamba Juice cup.

"Are you with the Trojan Whores?"

"Just Trojan Whores," Alistair said importantly. "There's no 'the.'"

In the studio, which was decorated to look like a fifteen-year-old boy's room, complete with a Lava lamp and Che Guevara poster, four wheelchairs awaited them. The idea was that they'd pretend to be decrepit during the interview and then wheel themselves onstage, leaping out of the chairs when it was time to launch into "Curb Appeal." Alistair wasn't crazy about the idea, but a talk show was a talk show. In their prime, the Whores had been interviewed exactly once, on a college radio show called *Sniffing Glue on KPYU*.

Instinctively, Alistair glanced at the ceiling, counting the tiles between sprinkler heads: the spacing was completely fucked, alternating between light and ordinary hazard. Clearly, they hadn't pulled a permit. He went into the bathroom and spent some time in front of the mirror, doing his best to become a Whore, fine-tuning his sneer so that it had the right pinch of irony. The trick was to keep the fear out of his face. Because this was it. Do or die. Or more accurately: Do *and* die. The music biz was kaput. The best you could hope for was to sell your song to Volkswagen. Alistair knew this; he wasn't naïve. Still, if the Whores actually went *viral,* they could blow up: Jimmy Kimmel, European tour, the main-stage festival circuit. They could squeeze in a last few years of fame.

The host of the show—a guy with a Cockney accent and a leopard-print vest, circa 1978—helped them set up their gear. He looked ridiculous. Maybe he was new to the country. For the interview, Alistair positioned his wheelchair between Glenn and Vladimir, who was staring at Glenn as if he wanted to separate him from his head. Andy slouched in the wheelchair beside Vladimir's, his eyes at half-mast.

"Can he talk?" the host asked.

"No," Andy said.

"He needs fifteen hours of sleep," Glenn explained. "It's like a disability."

"Love it," the host said in an American accent. "We can get a shot of him zonked out."

"At least he's not a snake killer!" Vladimir said. "He doesn't release juvenile pythons into the streets!"

The host giggled. He turned to Alistair. "Can you, like, act fucked up too?"

"What do you mean?"

"Pretend you're wasted. It'll be funnier."

Alistair blinked. So it was a joke. The guy in the leopard-print vest was playing a part. The name of the show, *Famouser Than You,* made sense to him now: this was a show that made fun of talk shows, or perhaps even a show that made fun of shows that made fun of talk shows. It was hard to be sure. The cameras started to roll, and the host slipped back into his persona, a washed-up "punk rocker" with delusions of grandeur. He claimed to be in a band called the Bottomless Assholes. Alistair felt his cheeks go warm, but both Glenn and Andy were cracking up.

"Was you ever on tour wif me mates, the Clash?"

"No," Alistair said.

"Wuzzabout the Vibrators?"

"We're from the San Gabriel Valley," Alistair said, making every-one on the set laugh.

Then the host introduced them, Trojan Whores, and they wheeled themselves toward the stage to take up their instruments. All Alistair had to do was get to the microphone. But he couldn't. His bursitis, fulfilling its imperialist dreams, had colonized his entire arm. It felt like someone had nailed it to the chair with a stake. He couldn't wheel himself at all. The host, thinking Alistair was playing along, pushed his wheelchair up to the microphone and handed it to him.

Andy, fully awake now, tapped his drumsticks together, and Glenn crashed into the first three-chord riff of "Curb Appeal." Around him, Alistair's bandmates leaped from their chairs, healed by the power of song. Alistair gritted his teeth, summoning all his strength, but he couldn't do it. The pain was too great. The mic smelled the way mics always smell, like a stereo that's been on all day—a faint whiff of singed cat—but this lovely smell didn't help him. He had no choice but to sing from the chair. He closed his eyes and imagined Naya watching him sometime in the future, once his humiliation had gone viral, kicking back in her new apartment with a computer on her lap, except the face he saw before him wasn't Naya's. It was a clown's. The one he'd seen on the motorcycle. The clown, in his enormous bow tie, watching him sing.

"They were laughing at us!" Alistair blurted on the way to their motel. His face was still warm; it was like a sunburn, only on the insides of his cheeks. Glenn, steering the van with two hands, bumped painfully over a pothole.

"It's always been a joke, right?" he said. "A laugh. *Mate,* we named ourselves Trojan Whores."

"I know! But we were the ones playing the joke on *them!*"

"Now the world is punk," Glenn said. "No one takes anything straight."

He was right, of course, which pissed Alistair off further. "I knew we should have hired a manager."

They stopped for dinner at a Mexican place, where Glenn spent the entire time reading his Bible, the same page he'd been on for days. Alistair's phone buzzed in his pocket, but he was too upset to answer it. He wanted the old Glenn back, the guy who read *Flipside* instead of the New Testament and stayed up with him till dawn, transmuting Alistair's dumb frantic longing into music.

"Read the part where Jesus mounts someone's ass," Vladimir said. He was still fuming about Stew. Andy, uncharacteristically, was sitting upright with his eyes open, sawing at his burrito with a plastic knife.

"You might at least try to converse," Alistair said to Glenn. "Be a part of the band."

Glenn sighed and closed his Bible, as if he were doing Alistair a favor. He hadn't once thanked him for saving his life. Who'd jump-started the whole tour and rescued him from a fucking garage?

"This whole reunion thing is for your benefit, you know."

Glenn met his eye for the first time. "*My* benefit? What are you talking about?"

"Look, we could all use a second chance. I'm not saying it wasn't my idea."

"You called me seven times in two days."

"I did not," Alistair said.

Glenn looked at Andy, who was air-drumming with his knife and fork. "Andy, how many times did Al get in touch with you? About getting back together?"

"Counting e-mails?"

Later, in the motel room they were sharing, Alistair watched Glenn gargle with warm water, something he'd done since he was a teenager. The Chateau Marmont it was not: hot and windowless and as narrow as a hallway, two beds crammed into it as if they'd snagged there during a flood. It smelled like a hospital ward. Adding to this impression was Glenn's sleep apnea machine. The mask was terrible, as large as a fighter pilot's, the tube hanging down like an elephant's trunk. Alistair had bought the thing for him because Glenn didn't have insurance. It had sounded like a blast, sharing motel rooms with his old partner in crime—maybe even gallantly helping him stay clean—but Alistair had failed to account for the Darth Vader sounds scoring his dreams from the next bed.

Alistair plucked out his contacts and dunked them in their miniature dunking booths. He thought about the first hotel room they'd ever shared, after the Whores had played Bob's Tiki Lounge in Sacramento. One of their first big gigs, opening for the Plugz. They'd dropped acid after the show and Alistair ended up at some runaway's campground, so wacked he spent an hour shouting into people's tents, weeping because he couldn't find Glenn. When he finally got back to the hotel and collapsed next to him, he saw a handwritten note taped to the ceiling over the bed. TAKE OUT YOUR CONTACTS, it said in enormous letters. Glenn knew he'd forget and wake up with them cemented to his eyeballs.

Alistair slipped on his glasses and checked his phone, to see who'd called him in the restaurant. He'd been hoping it was Naya, a wish like an egg, one that would hatch into being if he let it incubate long enough. But it was a number from Kansas: a telemarketer. He walked out into the hall and called Naya anyway. She did not sound thrilled to hear from him, though neither did she sound appalled.

"They played us on the radio," Alistair said.

"Congratulations," she said sincerely. He'd only been on the road for two weeks, but her voice sounded exotic again. "Did you and Glenn do that thing while you're driving?"

"What thing?"

"That thing you're always talking about. On tour. Where y'all switch drivers, going a hundred, so you won't have to get off the freeway."

"I'm practically a cripple," Alistair said.

Naya laughed. "I know. I was being mean."

He deserved this. It had infuriated him that he could suffer from something so clichéd as a midlife crisis, so he'd taken it out on the person who'd failed to save him from it. Once, after the housekeeper had come, Naya said, "God, I love it when the house is clean!" and he realized he'd known she would say this, that she said the same thing every week in the exact same way, annotating it with an ironic cluck of the tongue meant to disguise the fact that it *really fucking pleased her.* To Alistair, it was the sound of their souls dying. What he hadn't admitted at the time—even to himself—was that he loved it when the house was clean too. He wanted a sparkling house and somebody to blame for it at the same time.

"I miss you," Alistair said.

"Of course you do," she said. Then, more quietly: "Which part?"

"What?"

"Which part do you miss?"

Alistair listened to the distance between them, a seashelly roar. He'd made a terrible mistake, pushing her away. She was lovely, extraordinary in a thousand ways he took for granted, the only person he'd ever met who could use the word "weltschmerz" in conversation and also change the oil in a car. But he couldn't stop thinking of that squirrel on the power line, the sun-painted street after it was snatched away.

"The skylight's leaking again," Naya said sadly, giving up. "I had to get up on the roof and seal the flashing."

"Flashing?"

She sighed. "What are you going to do when I'm gone?"

Glenn and Alistair drove out to Claremont the next day. It was Alistair's idea. He'd asked Glenn to drive, not wanting to tax his shoulder before the show even though it felt fine. (Such was the nature of his body, unpredictable foe.) Sound check wasn't until five, and he felt like seeing his father's grave—at least, that's what he told Glenn—but the truth was Alistair had no great longing to see the headstone. He'd just wanted to go out there. With Glenn. He'd been envisioning it for days.

God knows what he'd hoped for, but the suburban streets and their tidy Spanish revival homes did not provide it. Hard to believe he and Glenn had grown up here, or that they'd been so desperate to get out, sweating around in the blazing sun with icicles hanging from their hearts. What had made them so angry? Alistair steered Glenn by the record store where they used to buy LPs, which had become a gourmet cheese shop. He got out of the van and peered into the window, as if Twig, the owner, might still be inside, blasting the latest Pere Ubu album. They used to ride their bikes here every Friday afternoon, jackets caped out behind them, to spend their allowances on records they'd never heard. The Weirdos, the Flesh Eaters, the Angry Samoans. The smell of new vinyl! The midnight-movie names! The first lovely crackle of the needle, as if the record were on fire: it was like the fuse before the song exploded. Even much later, when the Whores were falling apart, Glenn and Alistair bought records in Hollywood every weekend and then rushed home together, slitting the shrink-wrap with a fingernail because they were too impatient to find scissors. They'd listen to the album straight through sometimes, watching each other's faces, then start it again if it made them jealous. There was the Sonic Youth LP—*EVOL,* was it?—where the last track on side B had an ∞ next to it. It played forever: there was no groove to send the needle off the record.

Back in the van, Glenn was reading his Bible again, the same inescapable page. Was he memorizing it? Humbling himself like a retard? *Pay silent communion to page nine, and page ten shall deliver you from page nine, and henceforth on to eleven.*

"You could at least fucking *react,*" Alistair said.

Glenn laid the Bible on the dashboard. He didn't seem to give a shit about Twig's Records.

"What's that stupid page about anyway?" Alistair asked.

"You really want to know?"

"Yes!"

Glenn looked at him shyly. "It's the story of Lot. It's about how bad choices are cumulative—you know, how one leads to the next. First Lot *looks* at Sodom, then *moves his tents* near there, then *dwells* there, then in the end he's *sitting in the gate* of Sodom, a city official."

"I thought Lot's wife turned to salt."

"She does," Glenn said logically. "First he loses his home. Then his wife. Then his daughters get him trashed and seduce him."

"They date-rape him?" Alistair said, laughing.

"Basically." Glenn watched him laugh without cracking a smile. "My sponsor told me to read it every day."

"To remind you not to fuck your daughters?"

"To remind me that our choices have consequences."

Alistair looked out the windshield. He did not believe that bad choices always had consequences. It was a fantasy that adults had cooked up, to make them feel better about their boring lives. In fact, you could do everything right and still die miserable, just as you could do idiotic things—like smash your head through a pane of glass— and get off scot-free. It might even be the highlight of your life. Thus says the Lord of Punk. Alistair watched an elderly couple in Birkenstocks enter the cheese shop, which was named Gouda Vibrations. His old friend must have noticed something in his face, because he mustered a look of charitable nostalgia.

"How'd the phone thing go this morning?" Glenn asked.

"What?"

"The interview I set up! With *LA Weekly*."

Alistair frowned. He put on his seat belt. "They asked what makes the perfect Whores song."

"What'd you say?"

"You wouldn't be interested," he said.

On the way home, Alistair stared out the window, where a gibbous moon hung in the blue sky, faint as a fingerprint. What was it about L.A., that you could see the moon in the daytime so often? He felt strangely desperate.

"Remember how we used to switch places while we were driving, so we wouldn't have to get off the freeway?"

"Of course," Glenn said, unable to resist a smile. Inside of it was the old Glenn, glimmering like a prize.

"Let's try it."

"Ha ha."

"I'm serious," Alistair said. It seemed like a great and urgent thing. He unpopped his seat belt.

Glenn stopped smiling. "Don't be stupid. What about your shoulder?"

"Fuck my shoulder," he said.

"We're on the 210," Glenn explained. "You want a twelve-car pileup?" He pointed at the SUV in front of them. "Not to mention that. BABY ON BOARD."

The ghastly phrase, coming from Glenn's mouth, broke Alistair's heart. "You wrote a song called 'Infanticide.' Remember?"

Glenn looked at him in amazement. "Are you saying you actually want to kill babies?"

"How'd you get so fucking . . . *sensible*?"

Glenn shrugged, though Alistair could tell he'd gotten to him a bit. It was there in his eyes, as if he'd been pricked with a needle. "There are worse things to be," he said. "Like dead. As the Chinese say: 'Fear the wolf in front, and the tiger behind.'"

Alistair slid over till they were leg to leg and grabbed the steering wheel with one hand. They were going about fifty. Glenn looked at him with something like anger, then resignation, then a faint sparkle of excitement that narrowed his eyes into the old fuck-it-all squint of his youth. All of this in a one-second glance. He undid his seat belt, shaking his head, and Alistair stretched his left foot down to the gas so that their Chuck Taylors were side by side on the pedal. He could feel the toe of his old friend's sneaker. The trick was to transfer the pressure of their feet as gradually as possible so that their speed remained constant, steady as a yacht's. This required a kind of tele-pathic footometry. And they had it, Glenn and Alistair—it had served them many times, crossing the Badlands or the Mojave or the Great Plains of Texas.

Glenn lifted his foot, very slowly, Alistair stretching his left leg like a ballet dancer in order to keep his toes firmly on the gas. The speed-ometer dipped, but not too much. Then Alistair began to scooch over Glenn's lap, blocking his view of the road, doing his best to keep the van on a true and steady course while he squeezed between Glenn and the steering wheel. The problem was Glenn's belly. It was as large as a basketball and just as inflexible. Alistair tried to wriggle past but only wedged himself against the wheel, so close that he was basically humping it, sounding the horn now with his chest. When he tried to shove himself free, the van swerved wildly to the right. Glenn screamed. Alistair yanked at the wheel, righting it as best he could, still pinned against the horn—this was the end, the Great Hawk com-ing to pluck him from the wire—but then Glenn popped out from under him, freeing himself in the nick of time and leaving Alistair half sprawled in the driver's seat, unable to see the road, hanging from the wheel as if it were a trapeze, so that he hit the brakes without thinking and sent them fishtailing across two lanes before they jounced to a stop on the shoulder, triggering a fusillade of honks.

Alistair sat there catching his breath. His hands still gripped the wheel; he was afraid to ungrip them.

"Whoooo!" he said, though his voice came out small and hoarse. It sounded far away, even to himself. "Talk about stoned on God, hey?"

Glenn hit him in the face. A full-handed slap. Alistair touched his cheek, rubbing it so Glenn wouldn't see that his hand was shaking. The van smelled like burnt carpet.

Glenn retrieved his Bible from the floor, where it had fallen off the dash. "Why did you move out that day without even telling me? You stole half our records."

"I only took the records I'd paid for myself," Alistair said. "It wasn't stealing."

"I didn't know we were keeping track."

"I was unhappy," Alistair said gravely.

"So? When were you ever happy?"

That night at the Wiltern, they killed. If a few people were sitting, it was only from exhaustion. The songs were like holy water, the crowd begging to be sprinkled on. "Curb Appeal" had them pogoing in their All Stars. "Sex Is Boring" mined new layers of infernal sludge. "Traffic Report" had everyone shouting, "Northbound off-ramp is completely fucked!" as if it were their own song and the Whores were merely backup singers. For the encore, they did a cover of the Brains' "Money Changes Everything." The crowd wouldn't stop chanting their name. Even Vladimir was smiling. Drenched in sweat, Alistair squinted into the lights. The place was far from full but still looked crowded: a pond of faces if not a sea, the biggest they'd ever played to.

"Epic," the singer from the opening band said afterward, wearing a Trojan Whores T-shirt two sizes too small. The kid had cut the sleeves off, just as Alistair had done to his own shirt in the picture. "You guys kicked ass up there."

It was true, they'd kicked ass—so why did Alistair feel miserable? He heard the ringing in his ears, loud and merciless, like something that would follow him to the grave. His shoulder throbbed, and there was a new pain in his lower back, flaring when he walked. Vladimir and Glenn and Andy were breaking down the gear, still glowing with triumph. Mac from Merge had just asked them to sign an original pressing of *Trojan Whores Hate You Back,* gushing to them about the show and telling Glenn to be sure to call him on Monday. Alistair grabbed a Diet Coke from the cooler backstage and then went out to the van and climbed into the back. He rooted around the stray cords and boxes, looking for Vladimir's python. He had the vague idea he might wrap it around his neck. But the snake was still nowhere to be found.

He sat on the back bumper, then took out his cell phone and called Naya. She answered before it rang, which made her voice seem to spring from his own head. It was two o'clock in the morning.

"We brought down the Wiltern tonight," Alistair said. "They couldn't get enough. It was like 1983 in there."

Silence for a moment. "Was it everything you dreamed of?"

"No," he said. "I mean, it was exactly like it used to be, but nothing like the way I remembered it."

He wondered if he was shouting. His ears were ringing that badly. He'd called her, he realized, because she was the only one who'd understand him. Across the street, a boy with a blue Mohawk climbed into a Prius and blasted some hip-hop through the open sunroof. Another boy and a girl got into the car, laughing.

"Please don't leave me," Alistair said, beginning to cry.

"Because *I'm* the answer to your problems."

"Remember how we used to walk across the city, just make a day of it, from the Haight to Coit Tower, and we'd dream up the worst movies we could think of? That one about the pickle heiress and the small-town little league coach who fall in love, even though she's planning on selling the company and making lots of hardworking Americans lose their jobs. What was it called?"

"*A Pretty Pickle,*" Naya said. "God. Ha. That was an awful one."

"Anyway, that's one of the things I miss."

Naya made a sound he couldn't decipher. Somehow the sound—the sob, or whatever it was—contained the whole intimate failure of their marriage.

"So now you're starting to get nostalgic about *us,*" she said.

She hung up on him. Alistair sat there for a while, listening to the hip-hop booming from the Prius. This was punk, its true meaning and incarnation: fury and menace and a swagger to match God's. *Fuck you and your Hampton house / I'll fuck your Hampton spouse / Came on her Hampton blouse / And in her Hampton mouth.* It made Trojan Whores sound like the Wiggles. Alistair saw the boy with the Mohawk rise through the top of the Prius and stand on the roof, rapping along to the music. His face was bleeding and exultant. The hands of the damned yanked at his legs.

169

"That's one fucked-up teenager," Glenn said, appearing from nowhere. He glugged from a bottle of Jim Beam.

"Fuck are you doing?" Alistair said, grabbing the bottle from him. "You're not supposed to have that!"

"Too late."

The bottle was half-gone. Glenn wiped his mouth on his arm, already drunk. Alistair felt a sadness in his bones, like a weight.

"Fucking hell," he said. "Who gave it to you?"

"Some punk reenactor. A creative anachronist."

"What about being 'stoned on God'?"

"It was a great show," Glenn said grimly. His Flipper shirt was drizzled with blood, like old times. It was too late for Glenn—too late for keeping him sober, tonight and the next night and the next; too late, Alistair saw, for the whole carsick revival of their friendship. He'd convinced Glenn to get the band back together—*It'll be good for you!*—and he'd made his life worse. And Alistair saw his own life, the only one he would ever live, as an incurable thing, yoyoing between freedom and companionship. It was rock 'n' roll's fault, for pretending you could have both at once. He took a swig from the bottle himself.

"Give it here," Glenn said, grabbing the bottle back. He seemed angry and besotted with it at the same time. He swigged from it again, then farmer-blew one nostril onto the street. Graced by the old Glenn at last, Alistair found him much less appealing.

"So what did you tell that reporter? About what makes the perfect Whores song."

"I don't know," Alistair said. "The usual BS."

Glenn glared at him, his eyes narrowed into cracks. "Tell me," he demanded.

Alistair studied a cup of cigarette butts littering the curb. He felt strangely inadequate. "A few chords. Grabs you by the throat."

"What else?"

"I said it's like that first song that got your attention as a kid— 'Peggy Sue,' or something your mom turned up on the radio. It's that *feeling*, but crunched into the red."

Glenn nodded, hugging the bottle to his chest as if he were slow-dancing with it. "It has some mistakes in it. Don't forget the fucking mistakes!"

"That's what makes it good," Alistair said.

"Fuck good," Glenn said. "It has to feel like the best two minutes of your life."

"That's what makes it feel like the best two minutes of your life."

Glenn snapped his fingers. "And then it's over. Just like that. Before you even expect it."

Later, Vladimir drove the four of them to the motel, bouncing on his hemorrhoid pillow every time he stopped at a red light. Alistair helped Glenn up to their room, then deposited him on one of the beds and went to brush his teeth. Emerging from the bathroom, Alistair was confronted with Glenn's naked body. He'd removed all his clothes but had failed to get himself under the covers. Amazing, how time seemed to stop in the presence of a naked body, no matter what condition it was in. Glenn was flat on his back and yet his belly still looked large, weirdly autonomous, perched on top of him like a sleeping pet. His breasts, if that's what they were called, sagged to either side of him. His toenails were topographical: thick and yellow and rippled like clamshells. His pubic hair had turned gray. Alistair sat on his own bed but couldn't take his eyes off Glenn. Alistair's pubic hair was still brown. Maybe it was the bourbon sogging up his brain, but the white wisp of hair on Glenn's balls moved him deeply.

Glenn seemed to stop breathing for a moment, turning strange and red-faced, before gasping back to life. He'd forgotten his sleep apnea machine. Alistair got the mask from the bedside table and untangled the elastic straps. It smelled a tiny bit rank, like the sourdough starter his mother used to keep in the fridge. The hose was misted up inside from Glenn's breath. You could see the actual beads of mist. Kneeling by the bed, Alistair lifted Glenn's head with one hand and fit the mask over his face, snugly, and turned on the air.

In the morning, amazingly, Glenn was still there. Alistair had assumed, once he'd sobered up, that he'd go out at the crack of dawn and try to score. But he was lying naked on top of the covers, snoring inside his mask.

Alistair got out of bed, nursing a hangover, and shivered into his jeans, careful not to wake Glenn. His shoulder throbbed. He went to the van to look for his Advil. It was gray and foggy out, the marine layer carrying a whiff of salt. Vladimir, awake already and grinning like a maniac, was sitting on the rear scuff plate of the van, holding Stew's terrarium in his lap.

"I found him!" he said, beaming.

Sure enough, Stew was lying in his terrarium, coiled around a dead rat. He was beginning to swallow the rat's head, which was several times larger than his own. Alistair kept his distance.

"He was under the floor panel," Vladimir said.

"Didn't you look there already?"

"He was hiding under the spare. Happy as can be. Had to take the whole fucking tire out."

Alistair stared at the python, which as far as he could tell seemed no happier or sadder than before. How could you even tell the difference? Vladimir scooted over and patted the space beside him. Alistair sat down. Obligingly, without making a sound, Stew tipped his head back and began to eat the rat whole, shaking it painstakingly down his throat, hind legs sliding into his mouth until all you could see was the rat's tail sticking out like a demonic pink tongue.

The sun, shining weakly through the fog, warmed Alistair's face. He'd been appalled the other time he'd seen Stew eat a rat, but sitting there with Vladimir, watching the snake do his thing, Alistair felt a strange hush of relief. Nothing was expected of him—not even enjoyment. Stew choked down the rat's tail, bit by bit, as if he were eating his own tongue. He seemed unaware that there was an audience at all. Vladimir offered Alistair a hit from his vaporizer, then looked surprised when he said yes. It felt like a breath of sunlight. The snake dropped his head and for a long time didn't move. Alistair wondered if the performance was over, feeling suddenly ashamed, but of course it wasn't a performance. It was just his life.

RIGHT THIS INSTANT

On the night he discovered his mother might be a robot, Josh lay in bed listening to the Gutierrezes' beagle barking in the yard next door. Once the stupid dog started barking, it was all over. You might as well kill yourself. What else were you going to do? Fall asleep to its yelps, which sounded like someone was firing a staple gun into its ass? Josh didn't know what the beagle's name was, but he called it Crayola. Last month, his friend Bennett had reached through the Gutierrezes' fence and scratched the dog's balls with one finger and a little red crayon had popped, abracadabra, out of its penis. It seemed like Crayola had been barking ever since.

Josh touched his own balls, which felt sweaty and implausible. He'd only recently become aware of them as "balls," toys that dangled in a sack, and he could not restore them to dignity no matter how hard he tried. He told God that if Crayola stopped barking, he would leave his balls alone, but as usual the Almighty ignored Josh completely.

To distract himself, Josh focused on the gurgling toilet in the bathroom. The toilet had been fine until his mother's boyfriend had begun tampering with it, trying to improve its "siphon action." His mother's boyfriend was always discovering things wrong with their house, then trying to improve them. He had an app on his phone called iHandy. You couldn't walk into a room without finding him with his hands inside something, grinning like a maniac. First there was the toilet, then the garbage disposal, then the air-conditioning vent in the living room that had nothing wrong with it to begin with. Of course, the guy never actually did anything useful, anything that might actually *improve* their lives, such as smashing Crayola over the head with a sledgehammer.

If Josh's father were around, he would take care of it. He would get out of bed and put on his motorcycle jacket and walk across the street to the Gutierrezes' house, not grinning in the least. Through some magic expert dad power, the barking would go away. But his mother's boyfriend was a wuss. To begin with, his name was Timmer. This wasn't even a name. It was something between Tim and Timmest. Also, his face was orange. Not bright orange, of course, but definitely outside the scheme of nature. It gave Josh the creeps. And yet this guy with an orange tan slept in his mother's bed, and insisted on calling him "J-Man," and sprayed ant killer all over the house until it smelled like one of those vinyl shower curtains had been draped over Josh's head.

Yelp, went Crayola. *Yelp yelp yelp.*

Josh was losing his mind. Thoughts stuck to him and wouldn't unstick. He took a different tack with God and began groveling instead, pleading with Him to put the dog out of its misery. When that failed, he tried counting his breaths. The room seemed to breathe along with him, sucking in and out so that the dream catcher his dad had sent him from New Mexico looked like it might fall off its nail. The handwriting on the padded envelope had been strange and spidery. As he often did, Josh imagined his father driving to a reservation on his motorcycle and buying the dream catcher from a grave-looking Indian and then heading straight to the nearest post office, addressing the envelope against the wall, missing Josh so much that his hands trembled. The scar on his forehead was red from his helmet. The scar was shaped like a V, from when he'd smoked too much pot as a teenager and walked through a glass door. Sometimes, thinking about his dad, Josh felt such a terrible smashed longing that he wanted to walk through a door himself just to feel something different.

Other times he hurt himself for real. He'd take the screwdriver from his bedside table and stick the sharp end in his belly button and twist it as hard as he could, so that a precious bolt of agony shot into his crotch.

He had not told anyone about this. It was sick and demented and his dad would never want to see him again.

Josh switched on the bedside lamp and looked at the clock. 12:34. Was that possible?

He'd been lying there since nine.

The dog yelped. Then it yelped again. Yelping, it yelped and yelped.

Josh got out of bed finally and stepped into his slippers, which as usual he'd tucked under the bedside table, aligning them like actual feet. He crept down the hall, heading for his mother's room in the hopes that he could summon her attention without waking Timmer. Embarrassing to be wanting this now, at age twelve, but he couldn't help himself. He'd walked down this hallway a million times since moving to California, but in the middle of the night it seemed even uglier than usual: the place where his father had punched the wall long ago looked strange and conspicuous, sealed with ratty strips of duct tape. Josh's mother wouldn't let Timmer repair the hole— "material evidence," she called it—but Josh preferred to believe it was because she secretly missed his dad.

Come to think of it, it was strange that he could see at all. Someone had left the light on in the kitchen. Josh heard a voice, deep as a newscaster's, from behind the swinging door. Timmer's. And then his mother's voice, too, as if she were trying not to laugh. What were they doing awake? Josh couldn't be sure the voices weren't in his head, he was so demented with exhaustion.

He crept toward the door and cracked it silently for some reason and then stopped with it halfway open, peering into the kitchen. Terror glued him to the floor. Standing with her back to him, naked from the waist up, was his mother. Her back seemed to be ajar. There was no other way to describe it. Something was hanging open. A panel, like the door to an old-fashioned stove, except it was hingeless and Mom-colored and lined on the inside with wires. From the opening in her back, a perfect rectangle, came a darkness so deep that it seemed to hum. Grinning, Timmer approached the opening in her back and then stuck his arm inside it, crouching a bit to reach into his mother's head. His elbow twitched as if he were screwing in a lightbulb. He sighed and pulled his arm out and there in his hand was the strangest tool Josh had ever seen: a screwdriver, sort of, but crowned at the end with a tiny mechanical man, its face as marvelous as a person's.

Josh stepped back from the door. His heart was still. He was beyond terror and into something else. Later, trying to explain it to himself, he would think of *The Five Chinese Brothers,* the scene where one of the brothers sucks the ocean into his cheeks and leaves behind a land of algae and flopping fish. That was how Josh felt now, returned magically somehow to his bed: that the world he'd believed in for twelve long and trustful years had been sucked away suddenly to reveal a strange, gasping, impossible place. A thorn of vomit crept up his throat. Crayola yelped. Josh waited for someone to burst through his door, to tell him that what he'd just seen in the kitchen had all been a trick. *It was only a dream,* he told himself. When he looked for his slippers, they were tucked under the bedside table, neat as before.

"Morning, Sleepy," his mom said the next day. She was dressed in her Power Babe Tanning shirt, even though it was Saturday and she didn't have to work. Timmer liked the way she looked in it. As usual, he was sitting at the kitchen table and staring at his laptop, moving his lips while he read. "What were you clapping about?"

Josh shrugged. He couldn't tell his mom the truth: that he'd been clapping to alert them he was coming, worried he might surprise her and Timmer with their heads off or something. The clapping was mostly a precaution. At some point during the sleepless hours before dawn Josh had convinced himself that his encounter in the kitchen must indeed have been a dream. Perhaps he'd been sleepwalking. Josh had heard of such things: sleepwalkers waking up in the backyard or mowing the lawn naked or jumping out the window thinking they could fly. Bennett had told him a story about someone who'd taken a sleeping pill and then driven to another house and killed his mother-in-law, believing she was possessed by Satan. The barking could have had a similar effect, keeping Josh awake and unawake at the same time.

His mom served some pancakes to Timmer, who thanked her as if she were Mother Teresa bringing him shoes. The guy was like a full-time gratitude machine. You could kick him in the shin and he'd thank you for the learning experience. Incredibly, Josh's mother seemed to like this about him. After his dad had left, she'd gotten short-tempered and depressed and lost her job as a librarian at Josh's school. This was the Year of the Microwave, when Josh had to eat Stouffer's Swedish meatballs for dinner every night. But now she'd found a different job, at the tanning salon, where she'd met Timmer. He was a Power Babe Tanning regular, which explained the color of his face. You couldn't look at it too closely or it would seem weirdly afloat, like one of those masks you hold up with a stick.

Watching it now in the light of the computer screen, Timmer's lips moving silently for no reason, Josh felt his mouth dry up. The drained-ocean feeling returned. In his mind's eye, he saw the scene from last night perfectly: the panel in his mother's back, Timmer crouching to fix something inside her head.

Josh's mother served him some pancakes, then buttered them carefully with his knife. She'd done this since he was little, but there was something different about the way she did it now, making sure to butter every last inch, as if she were being graded on her performance.

"When were you born?" Josh asked her quietly.

"Nineteen seventy," she said, smiling. "Didn't you know that?"

"And the name of your first dog? When you were a kid?"

"What is this?" his mother said. "A school project?"

"I just forgot."

"Maybe J-Man works for Google," Timmer said, glancing up from his computer. He smiled at Josh as well. He was infuriatingly nice to him, in general.

"Buddha," his mom said, yawning. Her face had the puzzled, further-away look it had before she'd put on her makeup. She slid a pancake onto a plate and sat down with them at the table. "He was a shih tzu. Never barked at all—your grandparents, you know, actually cared about their neighbors."

"Now, Denise. It's not really the Gutierrezes' fault. They have a newborn baby to deal with. You can't ask them to debark their dog."

"I already have," his mother said. "This is war. Debark the thing, or put it inside, or I'm going to keep calling in the noise—"

"How did you and Dad meet?" Josh said.

His mother glanced at Timmer. "Sweetheart, I'm not sure what's going on, but I don't think this is how Timmer wants to spend his morning."

"It's okay, babe," Timmer said cheerfully. He'd been a flight attendant for a while and now did something with retarded people, Josh couldn't bear to remember what. He was only grateful Timmer had to work on the weekends. "This is a free breakfast table, last time I checked."

Josh's mother frowned. "He almost ran me over," she said, more to Timmer than to him. "In his pickup. I was crossing the street in high heels, on my way to a dance, and he didn't see me. My college boyfriend, bless his drunken heart, almost beat him up."

Josh felt a bit better, having confirmed this. He even managed to

have a few bites of pancake. Of course, you might program a robot to know all this—might even cram it with a lifetime's worth of memories. But would you program it to park its Honda Civic in front of the Gutierrezes' house and blast the radio out the window for an hour, just to piss them off? Would this really be something a robot did, even if it looked like his mother? The more he thought about it, the more preposterous it seemed.

"By the way," Timmer said to his mother, "the door gasket on your fridge is—how do I put it gently?—cracked. I'll pick up a new one on the way home."

He pushed his chair back from the table. Josh knew, by the pleased way Timmer's lips were tucked in, as if to make a popping sound, that he was about to use one of his special sayings. He knew, too, that the saying would rhyme.

"Well," Timmer said, winking at him, "this Boeing is going."

He kissed Josh's mother goodbye, leaning down and pressing his orange face into hers. Josh wondered what was going on inside their mouths. "Tonguing," they called it at school, which for some reason never failed to arouse him. Of course, this was not a difficult thing. The cashier at Hot Dog on a Stick; the palsied, big-chested junior at school who walked with her legs bowed in, as if she were gripping an apple between her knees; even the *Homo erectus* woman in his World History book, lifting a stone in the air and exposing the leathery hide of her breasts—Josh couldn't look at them these days without a sad creaturely stirring in his crotch.

And now, as he fought against this whirl of associations, something appalling happened: he began to get hard. Watching Timmer kiss his mother had given him a boner. Josh was so utterly mortified

that he swept his plate of half-eaten pancakes onto the floor, where it shattered into pieces, spraying the fridge with syrup.

"Joshua!" his mother said, whipping around. Her nostrils were wide as a horse's. "You clean that up! Right this instant!"

Josh barged out of the kitchen and then the house and then almost tripped on a sprinkler head poking out of the lawn before crossing the street and passing their car, which his mother had deliberately parked at the curb in front of the Gutierrezes' again. On the passenger seat, spread open like a book, was a case of his dad's old CDs. The October sun cooked his face. *Right this instant,* his mother had said. Josh had made her angry hundreds of times— thousands, probably—and he did not recall her ever having used this expression before. "Right now," sure, "immediately," even on rare occasions "pronto"—but never once could he remember the words "right this instant" crossing her lips. Of course, since his parents got divorced, there had been plenty of changes in her behavior. For as long as he could remember, Josh's mother used to tuck him in at night and do Steady Rain, Breeze on the Plain. It was just something they did together. He would close his eyes and she would lean over him smelling like white wine and flutter her fingers ever so gently on his face, up and down and all over. Then she would do the same except with her breath, a warm, tickling breeze that made his eyelids tremble. Josh had never imagined she'd stop doing this every night, it seemed as inevitable as sleep—but she had. At first he'd forgiven her. She was too depressed to get out of bed, and besides, his dad not being there had thrown everything askew. But now his mom seemed happy again, getting up early even on Saturdays to make pancakes, and Steady Rain had not returned. Josh was too shy to bring it up. He was too shy, as well, to bring up the quotes on his lunch bag, which had stopped sometime last month. The big book called *Bartlett's Familiar Quotations* had disappeared from the kitchen. The kids at school had made fun of him for the quotes— Josh had often secretly prayed that his mom would stop—but when he took his lunch bag from his backpack and saw nothing written on it, no inspiring words from Benjamin Franklin or Henry Wadsworth Longfellow, he felt a hole in his stomach, the same feeling he got when he lay in bed after a rainless breezeless tucking-in and heard Timmer and his mother giggling in her room, having what sounded like the time of their lives.

He wished more than anything when this happened that he could talk to his dad, but his father had his own girlfriend in New Mexico and almost never called. Instead he sent presents—or at least one present, the dream catcher. He'd bought more, but Josh's mom said he was waiting till he could deliver them in person.

Josh turned onto Yale Street, once again trying to dispel last night's hallucination from his brain, especially the ghastly tool he'd seen in Timmer's hand, when an awful thought occurred to him. What if the little mechanical man could come off its pole? What if, in fact, that was the point of it? With deepening dread, Josh imagined the little man crawling around inside his mother, replacing her with chips and wires, transforming her bit by bit until it could control her every move.

What if it was inside her, *right this instant,* steering her like a pilot?

Josh shook his head, trying to keep moving. He turned onto Harvard and began walking toward Bennett's house. All the streets in Arroyo Court were named after famous colleges: there was Columbia Street, and Dartmouth Street, and Princeton Street, and Stanford Street. Josh had never known anyone who went to college outside of Southern California—at least not in Rancho Bonito, where they lived—and mostly people didn't even do that. The desert sky was blue and cloudless, and Josh imagined it had been made by a giant Sky Machine. *Kerchunk!* went the machine and out popped another day, identical to the last one. All the houses looked the same as well. You could walk into any one and immediately find the bathroom. This had never seemed strange to Josh before, but now it began to feel odd. "Townhomes," they were called, which if you thought about it was "hometowns" in reverse. This seemed lazy and suspicious. If you were an alien building a fake town and populating it with robots, you might stumble across the word "hometown" and switch it around in your head. They'd moved from Vermont when Josh was nine—his father, God only knew why, having dreamed of living here—and in the Vermont that Josh had preserved for himself there were houses of all shapes and sizes and colors, a splendorous variety. Mostly he remembered clouds. He missed them terribly. They filled his dreams, vast floating icebergs in the sky.

And the snow! The snow, the snow, the snow. They used to go sledding down the timber road behind their house, staying out all morning until his father's beard was flocked with ice.

Josh turned onto Stanford Street, where Bennett was playing basketball in his driveway. He was five years older than Josh and yet liked to hang out with Josh as much as Josh liked to hang out with him, a fact that had only recently begun to feel weird. Josh had always imagined Bennett as being a popular seventeen-year-old—it was impossible for him to imagine an unpopular one—but after Josh's mother had mentioned something about Bennett's acne, how hard it must be for him, their friendship had gotten more complicated. Adding to this faint twirl of disgust was the fact that Bennett's parents had split up too.

"What's up, Tycho Brahe?"

Bennett sometimes called Josh this, even though Tycho Brahe was a famous mathematician who lost his nose in a duel and had to wear around a gold one instead. Like many of the things that came out of Bennett's mouth, it made little sense. He was stoned most of the time, so you just had to accept it.

"Why do you call me that?" Josh asked, emboldened by the volcanic pimples on Bennett's forehead.

"Because."

"I don't have a gold nose. I don't even like math."

Bennett stopped throwing baskets. "Fuck if I know. I thought you liked it."

"I'd like you to stop calling me that."

"Sure thing, Tycho Brahe. Whatever you say."

Bennett bounced the ball to Josh, who had no choice but to catch it. He was determined this time to make a basket. He had never made one before. Not just on Bennett's basketball hoop—on *any* basketball hoop. He was probably 0 for 70 or something like that. *If I make it this time,* he thought, *my mother is real.* He shot the ball from his chest, as Bennett had tried to teach him, and managed to skim the bottom of the net while missing the rim and backboard altogether.

"It staggers the imagination," Bennett said.

Josh sat down on the curb. This had so much the feeling of any other day—the blazing sun, the missed basket, Bennett's superiority to him in all things despite the material evidence of his acne—that Josh almost felt better. But when he closed his eyes, he saw again the little mechanical man, its face as perfect as a leprechaun's.

"You look like hell," Bennett said. "Your mom and her boyfriend still cracking jokes all night?"

Josh didn't answer. He wished he hadn't mentioned the giggling.

"You know what they're doing, don't you?" Bennett said, fetching the ball. "Trying to make a little Tycho Brahe. A bouncing baby boy. Out with the old, in with the new."

This had not occurred to Josh. He felt sick. The world seemed to stir around him, imaginary rustlings, as if he were being watched. Bennett pushed his sleeves up before taking a shot, revealing the burns he'd rubbed into his arm with a pencil eraser. They looked like miniature comet streaks. As far as Josh could tell, he was the only one who was allowed to see Bennett's arms. He was flattered but also offended that Bennett thought he was weird enough to admire them.

Now, though, Josh was happy to see the burns. They proved that Bennett was still Bennett: if you rubbed his skin hard enough, it would bleed. Bennett threw him the basketball, but Josh was too tired to catch it and the ball bounced into the street.

"What's wrong with you today?" Bennett said.

Josh's eyes blurred with tears. He was so exhausted it seemed like he might never get up from the curb. Once Bennett had told him, in a moment of stoned fatherly concern, that he could tell him anything.

"I think my mom and her boyfriend might be robots," he said finally.

"I know what you mean, Tycho Brahe."

"No, I mean they're not human beings."

Bennett shook his head. "Are they making you clean out the storage unit again?"

"No! Listen. I saw them by accident."

Josh took a deep breath and explained what he'd seen last night. He was afraid to look up when he'd finished. Perhaps the sky had split open and a giant hand was coming to pluck him out of the world. When he glanced up, though, it was just Bennett, nodding as if Josh had told him he hadn't made the swim team.

"Lemme guess—total dread?"

"Yes," Josh said.

"Goose bumps on your heart?"

Josh nodded. My god, had Bennett seen it too?

"Night terrors," Bennett said. "I used to get them all the time. Like a nightmare, but heavy-dutier. You wake up but it doesn't go away. I had this one, shit you not, where someone was eating my face. Holding it in his hands, like a cookie. I could hear him crunching through the bones. My mom talked to a shrink about them, I was so freaked out."

The relief was like a present. Josh would unwrap it slowly. Last year, he'd had something like what Bennett was describing, a nightmare so vivid it seemed realer than life: a vulture perched at the end of his bed, its wings spread open like a bat's and just as featherless. Josh had seen the silken clouds of its breath.

"They're not real?"

"Wow, you're really wigging," Bennett said. He put his arm around Josh's shoulder. "I've got just the thing, Tycho Brahe. How old are you now? Fifteen?"

"Twelve."

"Fifteen, like I said."

Bennett led him into his house and down the stairs to his room, which always felt like an exotic destination. Out of guilt or kindness or insanity, his mother had let Bennett have the master bedroom downstairs. In its hushed underground coolness it reminded Josh of a church: tapestries covered all the windows, so that they glowed like stained glass, and on the wall was a gallery of famous people who liked to use drugs, Jim Morrison and Pablo Picasso and Jack Nicholson and Lewis Carroll, the guy who wrote *Alice in Wonderland*. "Sailors of the psyche," Bennett called them. Leaning in one corner, propped up on a stand, was an electric guitar with a sticker of a marijuana leaf on it. But what never failed to enthrall Josh was the poster hanging over Bennett's bed, the one of a beautiful skier blasting through a mogul. Her ski suit was unzipped all the way to her belly button, barely containing her breasts, so that they seemed ready to break free of their imprisonment on the very next bump. Since she would never reach this bump, her power was absolute. Last week, Bennett had caught Josh staring at her and had made a V with the fingers of one hand and stuck his tongue through it. Then he'd flicked his tongue up and down. It was gross and electrifying and made Josh sort of want to zip the skier's suit back up to her chin.

"I've been looking for a Pope Leo XIII," Bennett said now, kneeling under a poster of Bob Marley smoking a joint the size of a taquito. "For my gallery. You know, he was a total cokehead."

"The pope did cocaine?"

"Kidding me? The Vatican was snowing like a blizzard."

He reached under his bed and pulled out the big glass bong Josh had seen him use several times before. The bong was tall, and purple, and the bottom of it was in the shape of an alien head. Bennett held a lighter over the bowl and sucked on the bong for a long time before lifting his face to the ceiling and chimneying out a slow stream of smoke, more than seemed humanly possible, such an endless stream that Bennett seemed to be deflating as he blew it out. It was like watching someone expel his own soul.

"Okay, Tycho Brahe. Time for your first kiss."

"What?"

Bennett held out the bong. "The Alien beckons."

Josh thought of the scar on his father's forehead, how his dad always used to boast a bit whenever he told the story of how it got there; he wouldn't actually grin but there'd be something in his eyes, an impish twinkle, like he and Josh were in on a private joke. Afterward, Josh's mom would look solemn and make him promise never to do drugs, and his dad would do his best to be solemn, too, but the twinkle was there between them, as if he and Josh were sitting in a classroom and his mother was the teacher. The air in Bennett's room, thick with sweet-smelling smoke, twirled pink in the glow from the windows. Outside were Stanford Street and Harvard Street and Berkeley Street, and then the car dealerships along Foothill with their balloons and pennants and dancing inflated tube men, and beyond that the brown desert hills filled with coyotes that ki-yied at night, at least when Crayola wasn't drowning them out. Beyond that, somewhere, was New Mexico.

He put his lips inside the tube. Bennett lit the bowl, smiling in encouragement, and Josh inhaled as he'd seen his friend do, the bong burbling like a creek. It wasn't until he breathed out that he realized he'd been taking in smoke. An itch burred his throat and he began to cough, gently at first and then savagely enough that he thought he might throw up on the carpet. Bennett took another turn at the bong and then handed it back to Josh, who thought he would only pretend but found himself repeating the same elaborate ceremony, right down to the coughing fit. He sat there for a couple minutes, waiting for something to happen.

Bennett flattened his hands so they looked like oven mitts. "I . . . am . . . a . . . robot," he said, jerking his arms up and down.

Josh astonished himself by laughing. Last night seemed like something from another life. How could he have thought it was anything more than a hallucination? He was too relieved, even, to feel ashamed.

"Me," he said, mimicking Bennett, "too."

"We . . . will . . . take . . . over . . . the . . . world."

"Oh . . . kay."

"Kill . . . all . . . the . . . children."

"Oh . . . kay."

"Ha . . . ha . . . ha."

Bennett lurched up from the bed and strapped his guitar over his shoulders and began to play it as if he were a robot, jerking his hand up and down so that it sounded like a radio tuning in and out. "Ev . . . ry . . . lit . . . tle . . . thing," he sang, in a robot voice, "gon . . . na . . . be . . . all . . . right." This was very funny. The opposite of Bob Marley was robot, but Josh had not realized this before. Josh laughed so hard his eyes watered. He could actually feel the tears forming behind his eyeballs, a region he'd never mentally explored but which he sensed as vividly now as the rug between his toes. The air was a haze of colors, warm and sculptural and *all right,* meaning every little part of it was right, and he began to understand why so many songs had "all right" in the chorus. The all rightness of the world was so well hidden that you needed to be reminded it was there. Feeling all right. Don't think twice, it's all right. Every little thing was going to be all right.

Bennett took off his guitar and laid it on the bed. He'd been laughing, too, but now his face looked different. It was pale and serious, more alert than before. Even his pimples looked less stoned.

"It is very amusing," he said in his normal voice. "The way you think we behave."

"What?"

"I wish you hadn't figured it out, Joshua. But you did. Your mom and Timmer were careless."

Josh laughed, but it might as well have been someone else's mouth.

"I don't know why I'm trying to save you from the truth. Operation Tycho Brahe is kaput."

Bennett reached up with both hands and clamped his head between them, one hand cupping his jaw and the other palming his crown, as if he were trying to snap his own neck. Then he gritted his teeth and started to unscrew his head. Bit by bit, as if in slow motion, his head began to turn. It was screwed on tight and evidently difficult to remove. Bennett—or whatever he was called—began to moan. After much effort he got the head far enough that its face was pointing over one shoulder. Josh could not move or speak or think. Fear had cored him like an apple. The room seemed to tunnel backward, elongating around him. The robot's head whipped back, magically, and broke out laughing.

"Oh my god. Oh my god." The robot was gasping for breath. "Sorry, Tycho Brahe. I couldn't resist. Your face was, like, too classic. I didn't think you'd actually fall for it."

Josh found that he had bridged the bed somehow and was standing behind it. The posters on the opposite wall looked like windows, a crowd of faces leering at him from outdoors. He fled the room and ran up the stairs that seemed to plunge toward him as he climbed and finally emerged into the daylight, which had the eerie partitioned flatness of a movie set. The cars, the sidewalks, the townhomes themselves—they were like a series of enormous backdrops with different things painted on them. On the steps leading up to Bennett's house, buckled like the folds of an accordion, was the shadow of a cactus. The cactus seemed flatter than its shadow, as if it were made of cardboard. Josh walked down the sidewalk as best he could, heading for home. His heart whistled with terror. He was trembling, and his throat was parched, and he had to take a dump. From the corner of his eye, he glimpsed a robot slipping into the Jayatilakas' house, carrying its head under one arm like a football. When Josh turned to look, the robot had disappeared. A sprinkler sputtered on and made him jump. Josh clenched his sphincter. Another robot scurried on all fours behind his mom's Honda Civic, but it was too fast for him to catch more than a glimpse.

The front door of his house was open. Josh tried not to think about the ramifications of this or what it might portend. He went inside and found his way straight to the bathroom. When he lifted the toilet lid he saw that it had grown white fur, like a rabbit's. The fur was the same color as the rug on the floor. There was a strange picture on the wall, a framed cartoon of a poodle about to drink from the toilet while a second dog told him to *let it breathe first.* Josh's scalp had turned to ice. He didn't dare move or make a sound. He sat on the toilet and closed his eyes, shivering while the pancakes he'd eaten for breakfast coiled out of him.

How long he remained in the bathroom he couldn't tell. It might have been minutes or hours. He'd stepped backstage—that was the problem. When he emerged, however, he saw that they'd replaced the furniture in the living room as well. There was a strange lamp with tassels on it and a TV as big and sleek as a sheet of glass and a doggie bed with the name TOTOPO embroidered on it. They'd replaced his mother, too, who was standing with her back to him near the stairs. She was plumper than she used to be and had black hair. One strap of her dress sagged down her arm, as if she'd barely gotten dressed in time for his appearance. She turned around and gasped.

"Get out of my house," Josh said.

"*Your* house?" There was something in her arms, pressed to her naked breast. A baby. Her eyes narrowed. "You're the Ingram boy, aren't you?"

Josh nodded, realizing that the woman was Mrs. Gutierrez. It was like a window flying open.

"What? Have you come to cut out Totopo's vocal cords?" Mrs. Gutierrez took a step toward him. "Your mother's ruining my life, did you know that? Think it's easy having a colicky baby and a jealous dog that won't shut up?"

Josh stared at the naked baby in her arms. It was a hideous thing, its eyelids so plump they looked like grapes. On the other side of her dress, darkening it like a bull's-eye, was a damp circle of milk.

"Don't tell me she's snipped your vocal cords too."

Mrs. Gutierrez pulled the strap of her dress up, easing the baby away from her breast. The baby began to cry. Mrs. Gutierrez rocked the thing in her arms, singing to it in a slow, pretty voice, a lullaby about one elephant and then two elephants and then three. The baby stopped crying and closed its eyes. The scene was so strange—the ugliness of the baby so at odds with the way Mrs. Gutierrez was treating it—that Josh decided it had to be real.

A man appeared at the bottom of the stairs, jiggling a finger that was plugged into his ear. He stiffened when he saw Josh and unplugged his finger. His arms bulged with muscles.

"What's Cruella de Vil's kid doing here?"

"It's okay," Mrs. Gutierrez said to him. "He's in shock." She turned to Josh. "What has she done to you?"

Josh shook his head. He wanted her to keep singing.

"My god, the boy's shaking. Camilo, look."

"Go home," Mr. Gutierrez said angrily.

"There's something wrong with him."

Mr. Gutierrez walked over and picked Josh off the floor even though he was too old to be carried and peered into his face, gripping him under the arms. His breath, warmer than the air, smelled of cough drops. The baby started to cry again and Mrs. Gutierrez resumed her song, singing even more slowly than before, each word hatching from her mouth like a bird. Josh felt as light as the words spreading their wings. He had not been lifted into the air in a very long time.

"Wake up," Mr. Gutierrez said, putting him back down again. "You're in the wrong house."

"What do you want?" Josh's mother said after opening the door. She'd actually stepped back when she saw Mr. Gutierrez standing there. She still hadn't put on makeup, which surprised Josh. He studied the words embroidered on his mother's shirt. POWER

BABE TANNING. P.B.T. Change the P to an R, one little stroke, and it spelled R.B.T.

But probably this was a coincidence. It did not seem likely that robots would advertise their robotness on their shirts, even in code.

"Your son has been using my bathroom," Mr. Gutierrez said. "Which is illegal trespassing. If I had to bet, I'd say that he's been smoking drugs."

Josh's mother laughed. "Joshua doesn't do drugs."

"I think your car confused him," Mr. Gutierrez said, ignoring her. "Parked, as it is, in front of our door."

He spat something into the bushes—a cough drop—then headed back to his house. Josh slipped past his mother into the living room, which smelled the way it always smelled, like Pine-Sol and perfume and the ant killer Timmer had sprayed into every crack. Something about the familiar toxic smell helped restore things to three dimensions. It was like Josh had been stoned all day, even before going down to Bennett's room, and was only now coming back to normal. He slipped past his mother, hoping to lock himself in the bathroom.

"What the hell has gotten into you?" his mother said, following him into the hallway. "You smash one of your grandmother's French plates and then sneak into the Gutierrezes' house? It's unreal, the way you've been behaving."

"Unreal," Josh said, facing the duct tape on the wall. The edge of the tape was frayed into little black threads.

"Look at me, Joshua. This is your mother speaking!"

He turned around and looked at her, surprised by the droopiness of her left eyelid. There was a gap in her lashes, a tiny pink stripe of rubbery skin. She'd gotten a sty there once and the lashes had never grown back. Josh was filled with relief but also a faint, mystifying dis-appointment. Once, in Vermont, he'd been driving on the freeway with his parents and had glanced out the window of the backseat and seen a car speeding along beside him with nobody in it, not even a driver; he'd felt a thrilling swoop of terror before realizing that the car was being towed by an RV. The world had clicked back into place, like the chain on his bike when he shifted gears.

"Do you remember my scab collection?" he asked his mother.

"Of course," she said, smiling as if she couldn't help it.

"Where did I keep it?"

"Under your bed."

"In a shoe box?"

"Yes. It was a disgusting box of scabs. Your dad wanted to flush them down the toilet, but I didn't let him. I fought your dad on that— I defended your scab collection to the death." She stopped smiling. "Joshua, what's going on with you today? Why are you quizzing me like this?"

"I'm not," he said, and realized this was true. He was testing *himself*, making sure his own memories were real. His mother must have seen something in his face, because her shoulders softened and she smoothed the hair out of his eyes.

"I know it's been hard on you," she said, "with Timmer here and everything. But I love you, sweetheart. Scabs and all."

She meant it—Josh was 95 percent sure—but it didn't help. It was no good. There was still that 5 percent left over. It would be there from now on, crawling around in his brain. He was the one who'd been tampered with, who wasn't the same. Even if she told him she loved him, even if she started doing Steady Rain, Breeze on the Plain again every night, blowing on his face as if she were tying a fancy knot with her breath—even if she did these things, a little voice in his brain would whisper: *She's just pretending, starring in a play called* Your Mother.

Josh turned from his mother so she wouldn't see his face. I turned from my mother, the voice in his brain whispered, so she wouldn't see my face.

Ev . . . ry . . . lit . . . tle . . . thing . . . gon . . . na . . . be . . . all . . . right.

"Oh my god," his mother said. She pinched his jaw with one hand and jerked his face toward her. "You *did* smoke something, didn't you? Look how strange your eyes are."

"They're not strange," he said.

"They don't look right."

Josh pushed her away, then fled to his room and locked the door behind him. It was the same room as always—gurgling toilet, dream catcher fluttering over the vent—and yet it felt all wrong, as alien as the Gutierrezes' house. Sitting on the dresser was the padded envelope his father had sent him from New Mexico. Was the wobbly writing really a sign that his dad missed him? Probably he'd just been in a hurry. Josh remembered the night he'd left, how he'd yelled and punched through the wall and gotten his arm stuck to the elbow. He'd cursed and struggled, the V on his forehead turning scarlet. It had seemed for a second—a terrible one—like he might never get free.

Josh lay down on the bed. He was so tired, so tired. Across the street Crayola tuned up for the night ahead. Josh didn't care anymore. He was too tired to move. His mother was speaking to him from the hall, rattling the doorknob. The miniature man in Josh's brain whispered: Ignore her. Josh lifted his T-shirt and pressed his belly button, holding it down with one finger. First his toes and feet. Then his legs and waist and arms. Then his lungs, his heart, the light in his head. He would not even dream. His mother, banging on the door, began to cry. Josh listened to her peculiar sounds, pretending he understood what they meant: *I'm human. This is a human noise. We make it from the day we're born.*

LAST DAY ON EARTH

When I was young, seven or eight, one of my father's German short-haired pointers had puppies. These were marvelous things, trembly and small as guinea pigs and swimming all over each other so they were hard to count. Their eyes, still blind, were like little cuts. After a few days my father decided we needed to dock their tails. He shaved them with an electric razor, then sterilized some scissors and had me grip each puppy with two hands while he measured their tails and snipped them at the joint. It was horrible to watch. The puppies yelped once or twice and then went quiet in my arms, as still as death. I didn't want my father to see what a wimp I was, so I forced myself to watch each time, trying not to look at the half-tails lined up on the porch, red at one end so they looked like cigarettes.

When it was time to dock the last puppy's tail, my father handed me the scissors. It seemed important to him that I do it. *Don't think too much,* he told me. When it came time to snip, though, I couldn't stop thinking and did it too slowly and there was a sense of cutting through something strong, like rope, except it was tougher than rope and gave me a curled-up feeling in my stomach. The puppy began to yelp and thrash around and I made a mess of the thing, snipping several times without finding the joint so that my father had to cut the tail shorter than all the others. He was upset. These were expensive dogs, and you couldn't sell one that wasn't perfect. Still, my father loved me back then and didn't make a big deal of it; he was planning on keeping two of the pups anyway, so he named her Shorty. He could do that in those days—turn his disappointments into a joke.

During hunting season, my dad went shooting once or twice a month, squeezing Shorty and Ranger into the backseat of his Porsche and driving out to a game farm in Hampstead County. I used to get up at the crack of dawn to see him off. He must have known I liked helping him because he always asked me to carry something out to the car: his first aid kit or his decoys with their keels sticking down like ice skates or once even his Browning 12-gauge shotgun in its long-handled case. But it was his Stanley thermos that seemed magical to me because my father's breath, after he took a sip from it, would plume like smoke. My mother hated coffee—"motor oil," she called it—and so I connected it with being a man. Often my dad didn't return until after dark, his trunk lined with pheasant, which he'd carry into the house by the feet. They looked long and priestly with their perfect white collars, red faces arrowed to the ground. It made me feel strange to look at them, and a little scared.

After we moved out to California, my dad stopped hunting, which meant there was no reason to keep Shorty and Ranger in shape. There was an old horse corral on the property we'd rented, and my dad set up

202

their pen inside it. Despite the creeping shade of an avocado tree, the dogs spent much of the day in the hot sun, snapping at flies, whimpering and getting fat. The corral was a good ways from the house, and eventually I stopped really thinking about them. The whimpering made me sad for a while, and then it didn't. I was fifteen by then. My dad kept saying he was going to find a home for them, but then he moved out himself and left my mom to take care of us—me and the dogs.

"We're going to the animal shelter," my mom said one afternoon. She was sitting at the kitchen table, holding a glass of white wine. I'd never seen her have a glass of wine before six o'clock. I inspected the bottle on the counter—it was half-empty, sweating from being out of the fridge.

"What?"

"I told your father that if he didn't come get the dogs this morning, I was taking them to the shelter. I've been asking him for six months. It's past one and he isn't here." My mother took a sip from the glass in her hand.

"They'll put them to sleep," I said.

"You don't know that for sure."

"No one's going to adopt some old hunting dogs. How long do they try before giving up?"

"Seventy-two hours." My mom looked at me, her eyes damp and swollen. "Your father won't deal with them. What am I supposed to do?"

My mother couldn't even get rid of a spider without ferrying it outdoors on a piece of paper. Then again, the dogs were unhappy, perhaps sick, and I certainly wasn't going to be the one who got up at six in the morning to run them up and down the driveway. I had no interest in dogs or hunting. The only time I ever got up early in summer was to go surfing, and I groused so much that my friends usually regretted taking me.

My mother poured herself another glass of wine, which spilled when she lifted it. She'd begun to wear contact lenses again, something she hadn't done in a long time, and her eyes looked naked and adrift without her glasses. On the kitchen counter was a book called *Unlocking the Soul's Purpose.* I wished my sister were here to see her—my mom, drunk and strange-eyed in the kitchen—but she lived in Africa, doing something for the Peace Corps I hadn't bothered to understand. She was nine years older, too worried about puff adders hiding in her laundry to care much about our parents' troubles.

I handed my mom a dish towel. "Dad's going to go apeshit," I said, hoping the swearing might upset her.

"Ha. Believe me. That doesn't even begin to describe it."

"Maybe he's tied up at work," I said.

"Your father doesn't have a job, remember?"

"He's starting his own business."

My mother laughed. "With his girlfriend?"

"It's a savings and loan," I said, ignoring this.

"Caleb," my mother said. "He's two million dollars in debt."

I smiled at her. "That's money he's *invested*," I said patiently. "Venture capital."

My mother got up to put her glass in the sink. My dad had told me all this a couple weeks ago, the last time we talked on the phone, but it was just like my mother not to understand. "Your mother's an idiot," my father said when I told him she'd described him as "unemployed," and what shocked me more than the word itself was how sincere he was—how calmly diagnostic, as if he were trying to make sense of his own hatred. As soon as he said it, I had a feeling like when you drink a Coke too fast and burp it into your head. There was something about her, something needy and timorous and duty bound, and it had driven my dad away. And now he would be furious about Shorty and Ranger—furious at me, too, for failing to stop her.

When they realized they were going in the car, Shorty and Ranger skittered around the driveway before hopping into the backseat. It made me both happy and sad to see they could still muster some excitement. My mother shut the door quickly, as if she couldn't bear to look them in the eye, and I remembered that she was the one who'd always groomed and bathed them when my dad wasn't running them up and down the yard, talking to them in a dopey, dog-brain voice that occasionally made me jealous. "Buster," she called Ranger sometimes, which is what she also called me, at least when I was little.

"We should do something for them," I said, "before we take them to the shelter." I needed time to think.

"Good idea," my mom said, looking relieved. "Where's the happiest place for a dog?"

"The beach?"

She smiled. "Of course. The beach. My god, I don't think they've ever been."

I climbed into the front seat while my mother shut up the pen. The dogs watched me eagerly from the backseat. Shorty's muzzle, I noticed for the first time, had begun to go gray. "You're not going to die," I told them, though they didn't seem worried. Already a plan had begun to hatch in my brain. My mother, trying to unhook the orange whistle from the door of the pen, dropped it in the dirt.

"Do you need me to drive?" I asked her when she got in the car.

"Don't be ridiculous. You haven't even finished driver's ed."

She managed to back the Mercedes successfully down the dirt road, even with the For Sale sign covering half of the rear window. My mother did not have a job—hadn't, in fact, graduated from college because she'd become pregnant with my sister—and despite my efforts at denial the new reality of our lives was beginning to sink in. Selling the Mercedes was not going to be enough to support us. The house had a tennis court and a swimming pool overlooking the canyon, and though I didn't know how much the rent was, I knew it was much more than we could afford. We'd given notice for the end of the month, but only now, watching my drunk mother back out into the street, did it occur to me she had no idea what we were going to do.

But I wasn't too worried. Not because I had any sentimental illusions about my parents getting back together. They hated each other, that was clear, and I was happy that no more dinners were going to be ruined because of it, my mother locking herself in her room to cry. But my father wasn't going to leave me high and dry. He'd told me as much after the separation. He'd take me in, if I wanted, just as soon as he found a bigger place. He was looking in Corona del Mar, trying to find a house on the beach. I could surf every morning if I wanted to. The name itself—Corona del Mar—sounded like a foreign country to me, a place you sailed to in a dream. Very soon he'd zoom up our driveway in his Porsche, bearing pictures of our new house, grinning in the way he used to when the trunk was full of birds.

At Grunion Beach my mother opened the glove box and fished out her old sunglasses. They were white and mirrored and hopelessly out of style, the kind you saw on the ski slopes with little leather side shields on them.

"How do I look?" she asked me.

Poor, I wanted to say. I pretended to drink the coffee I'd made her buy me at 7-Eleven. It tasted terrible, but I didn't care. I liked the warmth of it in my hand. We let the dogs out of the car, and they ran down the dusty trail before splashing into the water and then galumphing back out when a wave caught them. This was not the beach where I surfed. Homeless people came here, and spear fisher-men in scuba gear, and strange, well-dressed men with briefcases who looked like they'd walked through a mirror in London or Hong Kong and ended up at the beach by mistake.

It had taken some sly work to steer my mother here, and now I told her I had to use the bathroom. Instead I headed for the pay phone and called my father, my heart stamping in my chest. I'd never been there, to my dad's apartment, but I knew the address from all the letters my mom had to forward—*Now I'm his collection agent too*—and I pic-tured the phone ringing just a mile or so up the street, wondering if his girlfriend would answer. I'd tried sometimes to imagine what she looked like: tall-booted and glamorous and at home in the front seat of a Porsche, the opposite of my mother in every way.

When the machine came on and my father's voice asked me to leave a message, I was almost relieved. I explained what was going on, that he needed to come find us as soon as he could.

"Mom wants to murder Shorty and Ranger," I told his answering machine.

Down on the beach, my mother was absorbed in her Slurpee, suck-ing on the straw with her eyes closed. I'd been astonished to see her buy anything for herself at 7-Eleven, let alone a Slurpee, which she used to say would "rot my liver." Shorty and Ranger sniffed around for dead things, looking happier than I'd seen them in a long time. It was a beautiful afternoon—sunny and cool, with a breeze like a can of perfect ocean smell—and it was hard to imagine anything being killed.

"I haven't been to the beach in years," my mom said. She slipped off her sandals and dug her feet into the sand, and you could see the warmth of it spread across her face. Her sunglasses, when she tipped her head back, looked like a piece of the sky. "Believe it or not, we used to have a great time together. You and me. Ocean City, remember? We used to bury each other in the sand, like mummies. Your sister too. Even your father got a kick out of it." She shook her head, as if the fact that we didn't go to the beach together anymore was my fault. "I should have come down here more often."

"You still can," I said. "You can come here whenever you want."

She looked at me. "Do you really believe that?"

"Why not?"

"That I can skip down to the beach whenever I want, just for the hell of it?" She seemed angry, though it was hard to take her seriously with the Slurpee in her hand. "Nice try, but I'm going to have to get a job."

I smiled. "Like what?"

My mother lifted her ridiculous sunglasses. "You don't think I have any skills or talents?"

I shrugged. No, I didn't really think she did. She had an okay singing voice, nothing to write home about, and sometimes she could solve math problems without a calculator—but I couldn't really think of anything else, anything special about her.

"I see," she said, slipping her sunglasses back on. Her lips, damp from the Slurpee, looked thin. She gazed down the beach, where Shorty and Ranger were sniffing a giant bullwhip of kelp. "Remember when your father made you dock Shorty's tail?"

"Not really," I lied.

"I was glad you couldn't do it," she said, ignoring me. "It gave me hope for you."

I took another sip of coffee. The taste almost made me gag, but I decided right then to force myself to like it. Shorty and Ranger looked up from the kelp they were sniffing, distracted by a guy scanning the beach with a metal detector. He was wearing those stupid head-phones that beachcombers wear, moving his machine back and forth like a blind person's cane, so tan it was hard to make out his face. He waved at us, smiling, and my mom tugged the hem of her dress over her knees. I had never talked to a beachcomber before and lumped them in the same category as men who collected lost balls from the gully near the golf course, folks my dad called "bottom-feeders." I hoped Shorty and Ranger might scare him off, but the man walked up to them boldly and let them sniff his hand.

"Fine dogs," he said to me, taking off his headphones.

He was wearing a madras shirt unbuttoned at the chest, exposing a tussock of gray hairs. I'd heard the term "salt-and-pepper mustache" before, but this was the first time I'd seen one in real life. In another context—if he had been holding a tennis racket, say, instead of a machine for grubbing up lost change—you might even have called him handsome.

"German shorthairs?"

I nodded.

"Did you raise them yourself?"

"They're my father's," I said.

"Used to have a GSP myself. Frisky, her name was. She had hip dysplasia, so the name was perhaps ill-chosen." The man glanced at my mother, and I had the feeling that he was speaking to her somehow and not me, the way you might try to speak to a ventriloquist by talking to his dummy. He looked down the beach. "Where's your paterfamilias, if you don't mind my asking?"

"My what?"

"Your father."

I glanced up at the parking lot. "I don't know."

The man nodded, as if turning this over in his mind. He waved the detector in our direction, and it beeped so loudly that Ranger barked. "Sorry," he said, frowning. "Are you wearing a ring?"

My mother shook her head.

"It's attracted to you nonetheless."

She blushed. The man asked if we had a spot of water on us—"feeling a bit sponged out here today"—and astonishingly my mom lifted her Slurpee and offered him a drink. The man's mustache, when he handed the cup back to her, was red.

My mom laughed. She lifted her sunglasses again and perched them on her forehead. How different she looked without them: tired and sun-stamped, the corners of her eyes mapped with little lines. She was forty-five years old. Something in the man's face seemed to relax.

"We don't want to interrupt your beach hunting," I said.

"Not at all. I was just going to take a little breather." My mom sucked noisily at her straw, and the fact that she wasn't completely herself—that she was a bit drunk—seemed to dawn on him for the first time. "It's me, possibly, who's interrupting something?"

"Caleb and I were just discussing my talents," my mother said, narrowing her eyes. "Namely, how I don't have any."

The man regarded me gravely. The idea of her talentlessness seemed to offend his cosmic sense of justice. "Nonsense. Everyone has a God-given talent."

"Well, He skipped me. Didn't He, Caleb? I'm pretty much useless." My mom smiled at me, but there was a hardness to her eyes that I'd only ever seen directed at my father.

"I don't believe you," the man said. "Not for one second." He looked at me, then back at my mother, as if trying to figure out what he'd walked into. "You mean to tell me there's *nothing* you've ever done that made people go: *Hello, look at her, I'm impressed?*"

My mother cocked her head. "In college, I could walk on my hands," she said finally. "At parties they'd chant J.P., J.P.—that was my nickname—and I'd walk around like that. Once I even walked to class that way, just for kicks."

"There you go," the man said, vindicated.

I looked at my mother. I knew for a fact that she couldn't walk on her hands. She couldn't even keep up with her exercise video, *Aerobics for Beginners.* I had never heard her lie before, about anything, and it gave me an ugly feeling.

My mother glanced at the sieve hanging from the man's belt. "And your talent, I gather, is finding hidden treasure?"

"I have a certain knack," the man said, and winked at her in a way I didn't like.

"How does that thingamajig work?"

The man unstrapped his arm from the machine, which looked like one of those crutches old people wear except with a wire vining up the shaft to a fancy-looking control box, and handed the contraption to my mother. Then he slipped the sunglasses gently from her head and pinched the headphones over her ears and positioned himself behind her, gripping her hand with his own, leaning into her as if he were teaching her to hit a golf ball. The man showed her how to sweep the coil over the sand, back and forth. My mother laughed at something, and there was a look on her face I hadn't seen in a very long time, not since my parents used to get dressed up for parties and my father would tell her, in a voice I didn't recognize, how "radiant" she looked. She smiled as the man showed her how to work the knobs and buttons, asking him to repeat himself for no reason. She seemed to hang on every word. Though I had the sense, too, that she was trying to prove something to me, that the real her had stepped out of her body like the harp-toting angel in a cartoon and was watching me the whole time. I looked away. Shorty and Ranger were panting in the sand, exhausted from chasing waves, and I felt suddenly short of breath, too, and a little sick, as though I might throw up. A tire squeaked in the parking lot—my heart leaped—but it was just a lost Jeep turning around. Where the hell was he?

When I turned back to my mother, the beachcomber was still gripping her hand. She caught my eye suddenly and stepped away. Her dress was rumpled. She took off the headphones and handed the metal detector back to the beachcomber.

"How much does it cost?" she asked politely.

"Seven hundred," he boasted. "You can get cheaper ones, but not with a zero-to-ninety-nine target ID."

"What a rip," I said.

The man turned to me and frowned, studying me for a second. "Tell that to the guy who found the Mojave Nugget."

"The what?" my mom asked.

"Mojave Nugget. Four-point-nine kilos of solid gold." The man hitched up his pants. "You wouldn't believe the treasures lurking underfoot. Friend of mine, just last week, found a diamond ring, and no river rock either. One and a half carats."

I snorted.

"Pardon me?" the man said.

"Mojave Nugget. Jesus Christ. Don't be a moron."

"Caleb!" my mother gasped.

"Will you please just go look for pirate treasure somewhere else?"

The man was about to speak, to put me in my place, but my face seemed to make him reconsider. He straightened his shoulders. Gallantly, he handed my mother her sunglasses and then started back toward the water before stopping a few feet away to slip his headphones on, as if to show everything was fine. My mother wouldn't look at me; she put her sunglasses back on and plopped down in the sand again.

"Does it feel as good as you thought it would?" she asked after a while.

"What?"

"Calling someone an idiot."

I nodded, though it didn't feel good at all. My mother busied herself with her feet, swishing sand over them until they disappeared. I'd never heard her sound so disgusted with me. She yawned, and the disgust in her face seemed to shrink back into sadness.

"Okay, buster," she said to Ranger, checking her watch.

I glanced at the parking lot. "It's only three o'clock."

My mother stared at her missing feet, then at me. I remembered burying her in the sand in Ocean City, how my sister and I would cross her arms over her chest like a pharaoh's. It seemed like something from a different life.

"Here," I said, kneeling beside my mother and beginning to dig a trough.

"What are you doing?"

"Burying you in the sand."

My mother yawned again. "God, I'm so tired," she said. "Must be the wine. I feel like I could sleep right here."

I dug with two hands. The idea was to keep us here till my father showed up—keep us here, at least, until I could get ahold of him. The sand was less hot the deeper I plowed, each layer cooler than the one above it, and the coolness under my fingernails versus the warmth against my wrists was such a specific, one-of-a-kind sensation that I came unstuck from time for a second. I could half hear the shrieks of Ocean City, half smell the whiff of my mother's sun lotion, half see the smile on my father's face as he smeared the lotion into her back and made her hum like a girl. His wet hair was swooped back and perfectly parted—he carried a folding comb, one that popped out like a switchblade, even to the beach—and I found him incredibly dashing. One time, walking back to the car on the hard part of the beach where the surf had retreated, he stopped to show my sister and me the print of his sneaker tread in the sand, a perfect impression, complex as a tiny fortress. Embossed in the middle of it was the word ADIDAS in reverse. My father found this to be a marvelous thing. *Sadida,* I said to myself, because it sounded strange and marvelous to me too. And then my mother made a shoe print next to my father's—she was wearing sneakers as well, her old Tretorns—and we stopped to admire this, too, the four of us laughing for no reason, and I remember making the long drive back to Baltimore, feeling bored and lucky and spanked all over from the sun, and thinking *Sadida Sadida Sadida* as we chattered over the Botts' dots on the highway.

Now my mother lay down in the trough I'd dug, looking up at me in her sunglasses, and I started to push sand over her legs and arms and torso. I buried her as best I could. Shorty and Ranger watched me work. When I was done, she was a mound of sand with a head sticking out. Her cheeks, like mine, were dusted with freckles.

I let her lie there in her sunglasses, tucked to her chin, until I wondered if she'd fallen asleep. "Mom," I said, but she didn't answer. Then I jogged up the path to the parking lot, Shorty and Ranger trailing behind me as if I were leading them to the next great happiness. They waited by the phone as I rummaged in my pockets. I had another quarter, I was sure of it, but all I could find was a dime and a nickel. I checked the change slot: empty. I was fifteen years old—practically a man, or so I believed—but I felt suddenly like I might cry. I don't believe in psychic powers or anything like that, so I can't explain the certainty I had that afternoon, staring at the rusty phone and its rain-warped yellow pages dangling from a cord: a feeling beyond all doubt that my father was home, that he'd been there all day, that he was busy working and hadn't gotten my message.

I peered over the rocky berm to where I'd left my mother on the beach, but couldn't see her face. She was just a lump of sand. The beachcomber, too, was nowhere to be seen. I felt as strange as I've ever felt.

I checked under the rear fender of the Mercedes and found the little magnetic box where my mom kept a spare set of keys and loaded

Shorty and Ranger into the backseat before climbing behind the wheel, blinded by the leathery heat. There was a map in the glove compartment, tearing along the folds. I looked up my dad's street. The Mercedes started right up, no problem, and though I lurched a bit in reverse, I managed to get out of the parking space well enough and coax it onto the road. I spaced my hands at nine and three o'clock on the wheel, as I'd been taught to do. The big car seemed to glide along, responding to my thoughts. I'd dreamed about it so often that it was like I'd been driving for years. I pulled onto Palos Verdes Drive North, making sure to keep a three-second space cushion between me and the car ahead. I couldn't help thinking how easy—almost disappointingly natural—it was, this adult thing that all my life had seemed like magic.

I found my dad's street and turned down it, bucking over a speed bump that sent Shorty and Ranger tumbling from the backseat. At first I thought I had the wrong address. I'd been expecting a condo complex, but this was a stucco apartment building shaped like a box and propped up on stilts. It looked like it might try to creep away in the middle of the night. SAXON ARMS was written on the front in medieval-looking script. Parked under the building, squeezed between two of the stilts, was my father's Porsche.

I let the dogs out of the backseat and we walked around to the other side of the building, their collars jingling, and climbed the stairs. One of the apartments had a Beware of Dog sign, emblazoned with the picture of a snarling pit bull, taped inside the window. I stopped at my dad's door and knocked. It was not a long flight of stairs, but my heart was going as if I'd run all the way from the beach.

"Caleb!" my dad said when he saw me, nearly dropping the CD in his hand. He was wearing sweatpants and one of those pleated Cuban shirts with tiny buttons where there weren't any buttonholes, which I'd never seen him wear before. He hugged me in the doorway, and I could smell the coffee on his breath mixed with the chemical newness of his shirt. Music played behind him; he was a jazz fan—Fats Waller, that old stuff—and I realized how much I missed hearing its delirious ruckus around the house. Shorty and Ranger barked, excited to see him, and my father bent down to say hello, closing the door most of the way behind him.

"Did you get my message?" I asked.

"I did," he said, glancing behind him. "Just now. I've been on my office phone all morning." He cleared his throat. "Wow. Look at you. How the hell did you get here?"

"I drove."

"You have your license already?"

I nodded. My father eyed me carefully—suspiciously, I thought—and then treated me to the rare abracadabra of his smile. "Serena's taking a shower. She's been lying out on the patio. The woman can sunbathe through an earthquake."

The idea of her lying out in the middle of a Tuesday, instead of dealing with bills or laundry or groceries, seemed exotic to me. Scattered on the welcome mat was a pair of pink flip-flops. My dad bent down to collect them, grumbling under his breath, and Ranger slipped into the apartment. "Ranger, heel!" my father said, jogging after him. Shorty and I followed into what looked like the living room, though it was hard to say since the only furniture was a futon folded up into a pillowless couch. Nearby, tucked into one corner, was a kitchen area with a little stove and a microwave whose door was open and some

Vogue magazines stacked on the counter next to a Carl's Jr. bag. One of the cupboards had the sticker of a Teenage Mutant Ninja Turtle on it. I searched around for the office he was talking about.

"I've got my eye now on a house in Manhattan Beach," he said without looking at me. He grabbed Ranger's collar and pulled him away from a ficus plant in the corner, glancing at the closed door beyond the kitchen. I could hear pipes moaning inside the walls.

"What about Corona del Mar?"

"It's like Club Med down there now. Anyway, those cliffs? Whole town's sliding into the ocean."

My father turned down the music, then glanced again at the closed door of the bedroom. He hadn't thanked me for bringing Shorty and Ranger, but I chalked this up to my appearing out of the blue. Shorty found the Carl's Jr. bag on the counter and tried to pull it onto the floor, pawing her way up the cupboard.

"Down, girl!" my father said and yanked Shorty's collar, hard enough that she yelped. The dog skidded over to me, crouched on her hind legs. "No one cleans up around here. It's dog paradise. Didn't you bring their leashes?"

"I thought you'd want to save them from the shelter."

"I do, bud. I do." My dad's face softened. "But they're pointers. I can't keep them cooped up in here. They're run-and-gun dogs."

"Mom's going to kill them."

"It's me she wants to kill," he said proudly. He looked at Shorty and then glanced away again, as if he couldn't meet her eye. "Does she talk about me?"

"Mom?"

"We lived in an apartment about this size, in New York. This was before your sister was born. The boiler didn't work right, or maybe the landlord was just a prick, but we could see our breath in that place. Your mother stole some bricks from a construction site—a pregnant woman!—and heated them in the oven. We slept with hot bricks at our feet."

"Can't you keep them for a little while?" I said. "Till the house is ready?"

"I wish I could, bud, but they're not allowed in the building. Not even shih tzus. It's in the lease."

The pipes in the wall squeaked off, and my dad excused himself and disappeared into the bedroom. I could hear him talking to his girlfriend behind the door, the muffled sound of their voices—I imagined her naked from the shower, dripping all over the carpet— and after a while I had the ghostly sensation, watching the dogs sniff around the kitchen, that we weren't in my dad's apartment at all. From outside drifted the sounds of a nearby pool, the echoey shrieks and splashes, and I thought about when Shorty and Ranger were puppies, soon after my father had docked their tails, how he'd trained them to swim. We'd had a swimming pool in Baltimore and I remembered how he'd waded into the shallow end with them one at a time, cradling them in one hand and then lowering them into the pool that way, holding them until they got used to the water. They looked small as rats to me, their tiny heads poking above the surface. My father had them swim to me as I knelt on the deck—how scared I was that they'd drown!—but they made it to me eventually, trembling as if they'd just got back from the moon, and my father took them again and whispered something in their ears, clutching them preciously in both hands.

Eventually, my dad emerged from the bedroom with his girl-friend, who was fully dressed and drying her hair with a towel. She was pudgier than my mother, and not as tall, and had one of those dark tans like she'd stepped out of a TV set that had the contrast knob turned all the way to the left. She'd done up her shirt wrong, and I could see her belly button, deep as a bullet wound, peeking between buttons. She hugged me with one arm.

"I've heard so much about you," she said nervously, then laughed. She stepped back from me. "God, listen to me. That's just what I'm supposed to say, isn't it?" She noticed the dogs and went over to say hello to them, squatting down so they could sniff her hand. She scratched Ranger affectionately, just above the tail, and his hind leg began to bounce. "Aha. The way to every dog's heart."

My dad frowned at her, trying to send her a message across the room, but she didn't seem to notice.

"I thought they'd be more ferocious," she said.

My father snorted.

"Don't they kill birds?"

"Right," my father said. He smirked at me. "They have these little dog guns, and they shoot them out of the sky."

His girlfriend reddened. "How am I supposed to know? I grew up in Burbank."

She went out to the porch to hang her towel on the railing, and I heard a dog bark in a neighboring apartment. The one with the sign in the window, it sounded like. Shorty and Ranger began to bark as well. My father glanced at me, then cocked his head toward his girl-friend and gave me a secret look. He'd always been a mystery to me, a man of ingenious surprises, but now I knew exactly what he was going to do: roll his eyes. And that's precisely what he did. He rolled his eyes, one man to another, the only people in the world with half a brain.

At the beach, I parked the Mercedes and headed down to the water, Shorty and Ranger jingling behind me. I was jingling, too, my mom's keys in my pocket. The three of us jingled down the path.

My mother was right where I'd left her, buried up to her neck. It was four in the afternoon. A cool breeze stirred the sand, and you could walk now without stepping on the sides of your feet. I stopped a couple feet away, wondering if I should let her sleep, but then Shorty dawdled over and began to sniff her face. My mother started, then yelled at me to take off her sunglasses.

"Why?"

"I'm afraid to move."

I knelt down and did as my mother asked. There was something caught in her eyelashes: a perfect jewel, glittering in the sun.

"We can't afford to lose it," she said.

She shut her eye very slowly, like an owl, and I reached down with two fingers and plucked the crumpled contact lens from her lashes. Tweezed between my fingers, it really did look like a diamond. I cupped my other hand around it, trying to protect it from the breeze. My mother took some time getting to her feet, but I didn't complain. Anyway, this was our life now.

She found a Kleenex and we wrapped the lens up like a tooth and stuck it in her purse. My mother stared at me with one eye screwed shut, covered head to toe in sand. She looked less drunk, as if popping out of the ground had refreshed her somehow. Ranger bared his teeth and growled.

"He doesn't recognize you."

"Good," she said strangely. She brushed the sand from her arms and legs as best she could and squinted one-eyed down the beach.

"He's gone," I said.

She nodded. The breeze had sharpened to a wind and the waves were getting blown out, dark patches flickering across the water and misting the tops of them. You could smell the salt in the air, stronger than before. My mother bent down and rubbed her legs, which were covered in goose bumps.

"It's getting chilly out here," she said. She closed both eyes for a moment, as if she were feeling woozy. "Can I have some of your coffee?"

I went over and grabbed the cup of cold coffee from the sand and handed it to her. She took a sip and grimaced.

"You really like this stuff?"

"No," I said. I handed her the sunglasses.

"You might like it in a couple years."

I tried to imagine what I'd look like in a couple years, and where we'd be living, and how the hell my mother would manage to support us. I tried to imagine this, but I couldn't. I looked toward the water and could see the curve of the earth, way out where the ocean faded into a strip of white, a lone barge out there shimmering on the horizon, still and dainty as a toy, and for a moment the wind at my shirt seemed to blow right through me.

My mother poured the dregs of her Slurpee out, and the dogs sniffed over to the damp spot in the sand, bumping noses. My mom watched them for a while, pink already with sunburn, her glasses reflecting a smaller version of the world, as if the beach and crashing waves and vacant lifeguard stand were as far away as that boat on the horizon, and I could see why Ranger had barked at her. She looked unrecognizable to me too.

"Why did you say that to that beachcomber?" I asked.

"Which part?"

"That you can walk on your hands?"

My mother looked at me humbly. Then she walked toward the water where the sand was firmer. She got down on all fours and jumped her legs up so she was standing on her hands, bent like a scorpion's tail, the skirt of her dress hanging down around her. You could see her underwear—plain as a man's briefs—but at the moment I was too astounded to care. She walked that way for a few steps, teetering along on her hands and scaring up a puff of kelp flies. A wave foamed between her fingers, dampening the ends of her hair, but she didn't stop. I had the sense that this was the only time I'd ever see her do this. After today, we wouldn't have the chance. But she could still do it now, she could surprise me with a useless talent. The sun flashed behind her, flickering between her legs, and someone watching from down the beach might even have mistaken us for two kids. She teetered on like that, on the verge of falling, while Shorty and Ranger barked and splashed around her, wagging their stubby little tails, no idea what was next.

ACKNOWLEDGMENTS

Thanks to the American Academy of Arts and Letters, the Jeannette Haien Ballard trust, the MacDowell Colony, the literature department at Claremont McKenna College, and The Writing Seminars at Johns Hopkins University for their generous support during the writing of this book. Thanks, too, to the many people who helped me with these stories: Tom Barbash, Neil Eber, Matt Klam, Greg Martin, Tom McNeely, Jeff O'Keefe, Dan Stolar, Kenny Wachtel, and especially Andrew Altschul and Scott Hutchins. I'm grateful to all the magazines and editors who ushered these stories into print, particularly Cheston Knapp at *Tin House*, who pushed me to make several of them better and always seemed eager to read the next thing. Thanks to my fantastic editor, Kara Watson, for her advocacy and expertise, and to Nan Graham for all her support. I wouldn't have been able to write this book without the friendship, guidance, and encouragement of my agent, Dorian Karchmar, who read each of these stories many times and helped them find their way into the world. She's a gift from the lonely-writer gods and I can't thank her enough. Finally, thanks to Katharine Noel, love of my life, who took time from her own work to read every single draft of these stories and whose true way of seeing the world helped inspire them to begin with.